# TO WEAVE A
# TANGLED WEB

# TO WEAVE A
# TANGLED WEB

Patrick R. Condon

| Library of Congress Control Number: | | 2011917061 |
|---|---|---|
| ISBN: | Hardcover | 978-1-4653-6982-6 |
| | Softcover | 978-1-4653-6981-9 |
| | Ebook | 978-1-4653-6983-3 |

**To order additional copies of this book, contact:**
Xlibris Corporation
1-888-795-4274
www.Xlibris.com
Orders@Xlibris.com
102607

In

memory of

The Twerpe-Zoid.

Loving friend

for fifteen years.

He sat on my

lap and purred

during the writing

of this book,

but passed away

one day before

its completion.

# ACKNOWLEDGEMENTS

To Lynn deBeauclair, my good friend and editor, for her patient editing of my punctuation, grammar, spelling, and other occasional glitches. Primarily from our back and forth editing procedure, because her Mac and my PC were often in dispute.

For his inspiration when I was a child reading his books under the covers with a flashlight, and again as an adult when I was declared disabled and remembered that Robert A. Heinlein had said, "They told me I was disabled. So, I decided that if I couldn't do honest work anymore, I would just have take up writing." My thanks to the late Mr. Heinlein and his family.

All three of my siblings, J, T, and T. You have all been there for me throughout my life.

# PERSONIS

**Human:**
*Democratic Earth Societies:*
Lao Chin - President of DES
Gerry - Aide to Lao Chin
Mandy Frost - Minister of Foreign Relations
Robert Clarke - Minister of War
Habib Assad - Minister of Science
Court Maltese - Minister of Security
Admiral Christopher Price - DES Nimitz
Admiral Wyzincski - DES
Captain Vaugn Hiemler - DES Bismarck
Captain Randolph Leonard - DES Stephen Hawking
First Officer Abe Mathews - DES Stephen Hawking
Commander Alexi Adreiovich - DES Bismarck
Commander David Farmer - DES Bismarck
Engineer First Class Anuk - DES Stephen Hawking
Engineer Second Class Michael Hotchkins - DES Stephen Hawking
Flight Chief Phillipe D'Amato - DES Nimitz

*Confederated Human Colonies:*
Allison Susan McCallister - President of CHC
Sing - Aide to Allison McCallister
Leo Walsh - Vice President
Artemus O'Toole - Science Advisor
Admiral Seamus Hurley
Admiral Jefferson Brave Eagle
Captain Robert Black Elk - CHC/DES Sitting Bull
Chief Katy O'Shea - Lagrange Five Space Station (Near Memory Beta)

**Fombe:**
Shidig - Overall Clan Leader
Brak - Ambassador to the Galactic Council
Admiral Mailiew Rentahs - Fleet Commander and Commander of the Ttiflan
Pomb - Captain Ttiflan
Skarl - Science Officer Ttiflan
Mulci - Second Shift Physician Ttiflan
Tserofed - Yeoman Ttiflan

**<u>Binqk:</u>**
Emperor Pishmah Umselat Bourbaitoo III
Mek - Ambassador to the Galactic Council
Chok - Special Representative to the Fombe
Eenvupe - Admiral 1st Fleet
Hutspa - Captain 1st Fleet
Papum - Admiral 2nd Fleet

**<u>Pilok:</u>**
Bakstrah - Engineer for Pilok Ambassador

# CHAPTER 1

In a lavish office equipped with all the latest in communications equipment and high tech computers, deep inside a mountain called Cheyenne in the former State of Colorado a member of the former United States of America, a recording was being played. The audience was an extremely somber group of officials.

"I repeat! We are under attack from an unknown source without warning or provocation. Their ships do not match any known human design. We can only assume that they are extra-terrestrial in origin."

There were a few seconds of static-enhanced silence from the recording device then, "already done for" then all those listening heard, "They have already bombed the planet bound colony. I doubt that anyone survived the assault. Planetary defenses were nearly nonexistent and overwhelmed immediately. I do not believe our space habitat can survive another barrage and they refuse to answer any friendship messages. I have sent all the sensor data we have on them . . . Wait! Oh, God! No!" There was a loud explosive sound accompanied by the agonized scream of tearing and rending metal, the "whoosh" of escaping air, and then only background static.

"That is the end of the message, Mr. President," Minister of War Robert Clarke, stated flatly.

President Lao Chin, of the Democratic Earth Societies, was pale and his voice quavered as he asked, "How many people Bob?"

"Approximately forty five thousand between the space habitat and the planet-based colony, Mr. President."

"Dear God," Chin muttered quietly. Suddenly, he looked and felt much older than his true age. Not quite considered elderly yet, he was only 98 standard years old. His hair was only beginning to gray and his mind still quite sharp. His days of playing tennis might be over, but he could still engage in less demanding physical exercise.

"OK, now what should we do? Have we heard anything from the other colonies?"

"No, Mr. President, no other colonies have reported being attacked if that is what you mean," replied the Minister of Foreign Relations, Mandy Frost.

"No, I mean have any of them claimed responsibility?" demanded Chin.

"Mr. President," began Clarke, "the sensor data and the statements in the transmission both show that the attacking vessel was not of human origin. Therefore, we conclude that they were indeed alien in both nature and origin."

"I concur with that, Mr. President." That from Minister of Science Habib Assad. "All of the available data points to an alien race."

"How can that be?" asked Chin. "We have created thirty three colonies, and our colonies have produced twelve other colonies. How is it we never encountered another sapient species before this? And why would they attack?"

"As for how come we haven't met them before, Mr. President," said Assad, "it is a big galaxy."

"As for the why, only one thing is certain," this from Clarke. "It means we are at war. I highly recommend we send an investigative team to find out as much as we can about the enemy."

"You are, of course, correct Bob. But take some of Assad's folks with you. Mandy, I want you to send someone from your department as well. Maybe we can settle this thing quietly and peacefully. That will be all for now. This meeting is adjourned."

As the others filed out of the room, President Chin placed his head in his hands and tried to steady his nerves. An alien race, an attack without warning or provocation, and a new war with he knew not who or what. This was certainly not starting out as one of the better days in his term of office.

# CHAPTER 2

Aboard the Fombe cruiser Ttiflan, Admiral Rentahs was making final preparations to depart when he received a call saying that Ambassador Brak himself requested a secure communication link.

The admiral chose to take the link in his cabin. The holo picture was better and Brak did not call fleet admirals. Privacy seemed advisable.

"Greetings, Admiral Rentahs. Honor and warmth to your bed and all of the seed planted there."

"And to yours, Mr. Ambassador." The formal greeting presented could only mean that this was to be an official and therefore important conference. Rentahs readied himself for a new problem to be dealt with. "How may I be of service to you, Mr. Ambassador?"

"Before I answer that Admiral, have you been briefed on your mission?"

"Yes, my ships and I will be ready to depart in three chron clicks."

"Admiral, this may seem a bit unusual, but I must ask. Would you please give me a brief synopsis of your mission? The political climate about this mission is extremely delicate, therefore I must know exactly what your mission is."

"Of course Mr. Ambassador. In brief, I am to proceed to the system designated as Psht Phas Five, the fourth planet in the system, and investigate. Once there, I am to determine if an attack happened and if so, attempt to determine who the attackers were as well as who was attacked. If it turns out that those attacked were indeed not a member of the Galactic Council of Sapient Space-going Species, I am to make a discreet investigation and attempt to locate the home planet of the race. At no time am I to take any aggressive action against this species. I will then return and report to you directly. From there, I am to stand ready to testify before the Emperor and/or the Galactic Council as required."

"Excellent, Admiral. Thank you. But now I need to introduce a new, 'difficulty' to your mission."

Rentahs steadied himself thinking, "Here it comes."

"Because of the nature of this mission and the fact that it directly involves the Binqk, they have requested, and the Galactic Council agreed, that they should have a representative accompany you on your mission." Several seconds of silence followed during which Admiral Rentahs showed no outward change and said nothing. Inside his own mind however, Rentahs posed a set of invectives, curses, colorful metaphors, and outright swear words that if put to print might well win him an artist's award from the State. He did not, however. It would be unseemly for an admiral to do so, especially when in reference to a state dignitary.

Brak was well aware of the emotions going on inside the admiral. He knew the type of revulsion the Binqk caused in his people and how unsettling their violent nature could be. He allowed time for the admiral to absorb and deal with the information before proceeding. Eventually the admiral would speak up.

"Mr. Ambassador," Rentahs finally said, "surely you know the types of problems this will cause aboard ship."

"I do sir, but it is out of our control. The Galactic Council has determined it is to be so. I apologize, but I cannot do anything to change it. You have my sympathies, Admiral."

"Thank you, Mr. Ambassador."

"The representative of the Binqk is due to arrive at your location within the next two chron clicks. Again, I apologize. I would have liked to give you more time to prepare for the Binqk's arrival, but the situation is what it is and we must learn to deal with it.

"Good luck, Admiral Rentahs."

"May your bed always be full of friends and comfortably warm, Ambassador Brak."

To a race such as the Fombe, whose culture and lives revolved around being able to breed successfully, the very notion of a race without gender such as the Binqk was revolting. The fact that the Binqk took great pride in their lack of gender made them even less tolerable and more disgusting.

The Binqk's violent tendencies and aggressive nature made them nearly intellectually incompatible to the Fombe, a race that prided itself on personal responsibility, intellectual achievements, and overcoming their aggressive instincts.

So, when the Binqk representative arrived seven chron clicks late, Admiral Rentahs was more than irritated and therefore allowed Captain Pomb to greet the Binqk special representative. It was as close to a personal insult without actually being one that Rentahs could get.

"*Captain* Pomb?" inquired the Binqk special representative. "Considering the nature of this mission and my own importance to it, I expected Admiral Rentahs to greet me personally."

"The Admiral sends his apologies. Ship's business has kept him away," replied Pomb.

"'Ship's business' indeed!" the creature growled, then raised its voice, "I am Special Representative Chok of the Binqk Empire. This breach of etiquette is insulting to say the least. I do trust it will not continue. I do not take kindly to being insulted."

"*Sir*," Captain Pomb used the gender specific term in a carefully neutral manner the translator couldn't possibly interpret. "No insult was intended. I apologize if it seems so. May I escort you to your quarters?"

"That at least is acceptable. And I will meet with your Admiral Rentahs immediately afterward."

The communications panel chimed softly for attention. Rentahs touched a control and Captain Pomb appeared on the screen.

"Admiral, Special Representative Chok will meet with you," a tiny pause, then *now*," Pomb said somewhat too politely.

"He will meet with me *now*?" exclaimed Rentahs. "Does Chok think this is a Binqk ship? That it, is in command?"

"My apologies, Admiral," deferred Pomb.

Rentahs could tell that Pomb was also furious with the arrogant Binqk, and he was guilt ridden over taking out his frustration on an officer who had already had to deal with the disgusting creature. "No. My apologies, Captain Pomb. You have performed your duties above and beyond the call of duty. Fault does not lie upon your shoulders. These Binqk can be most infuriating. I will contact Chok myself and attempt to ease its mind. Thank you, Captain. That will be all."

Admiral Rentahs took a few minutes to compose himself and then contacted Chok via standard ship's communications. "Special Representative Chok, I greet you warmly. Welcome aboard the Ttiflan."

"Admiral Rentahs. Kind of you to call, if not visit in person."

"Chok," continued Rentahs avoiding the verbal jab, "we are ready to depart. I wanted to make sure you were comfortable before we do so."

"Well then, Admiral," Chok said, "since you ask, am I to be confined to these quarters or an environmental suit for the entire voyage?"

"My apologies. But you cannot expect me to make my entire crew of nearly one thousand Fombe wear environmental suits on board their own ship, just to accommodate you. It would be impractical as well as dangerous to the mission."

"'Dangerous to the mission!' I wonder if you really understand the significance of this mission, Admiral."

"Sir," Rentahs intentionally used the gender specific term to create as much insult as possible without actually insulting this pompous creature, "I am well aware of the significance of this mission and the possible repercussions. I will contact you as soon as we have arrived at system Psht Phas Five. Rentahs out."

With that, he disconnected the communication link before Chok could make any more objections or insults.

"Communications," ordered the Admiral, "contact the Catchiflan and Xyflan. Inform them we are ready to depart. Captain Pomb, commence acceleration to the incursion point. When the fleet is ready, make the jump at your own discretion."

"You have the conn Captain. I will be in my quarters."

# CHAPTER 3

It was a small system with a small star. Names are not important. This particular star was currently known by over two hundred thousand names depending on who or what you asked. In times past it had been known by over one hundred million names to species now long extinct.

High above the ecliptic plane of the system something out of the ordinary was happening. Space seemed to be folding in on itself. Not a rip exactly, more of a carefully sculptured hole seemed to form. The hole turned into a tunnel. Then, from within that tunnel, something arrived.

The battleship DES Bismarck made the incursion into normal space. She hung there watching, listening. Two minutes later there was another normal space incursion and the carrier Nimitz appeared, followed seven minutes after that by the science ship Stephen Hawking. All three ships hung silently in the dark, almost as if they were predators awaiting prey to show up at a watering hole.

Aboard the Nimitz, Fleet Admiral Christopher Price barked, "Get me Captain Hiemler on the Bismarck and Captain Leonard on the Hawking." A tall muscular man with graying hair and the scars of two previous wars, his manner and voice left no doubt he was used to being instantly obeyed without question.

Within seconds the main viewer showed the image of Captain Vaugn Hiemler. Short with blonde hair, blue eyes, and of indeterminate age he had a menacing look about him that left many an ensign shaking nervously for hours after a good dressing down.

"Report, Vaugn." Price stated simply.

"Sir, as per orders, we have not used any but the passive sensors since arrival. Nothing out of the ordinary to report at this time."

The screen split in two as the image of Captain Randolph Leonard of the science ship DES Stephen Hawking appeared on the screen.

Captain Leonard looked at the pickup and said, "Admiral?"

"Report!" demanded Price.

"I am trying to provide you with one now, Sir. Mr. Matthews, report!"

A small mousey looking fellow peered at him over the top of old fashioned glasses. "We have nothing to report yet, Captain. We have only now unlimbered our sensor array and have not activated any but the passive sensors, as per your order. But the Bismarck's passive sensors are as good as ours and they have had more time to examine the area. Have they discovered anything we should be aware of?"

Price shifted in his command chair and clamped down on the caustic remark he wanted to make. He hated working with scientists. They were so oblivious of military protocol. Nonetheless, in this mission they were not only invaluable but absolutely necessary.

"Captain Leonard," he began impatiently, "since we have gained no information from passive scans of the system, I authorize you to go to full scanning capability. However, you will inform me the instant you have something relevant to report. Out."

"Captain Hiemler, bring the Bismarck to full active status. Maintain yellow alert readiness and be prepared to go to full battle alert at a moment's notice. Out."

"Comm, get me Flight Chief D'Amato. Science, activate full sensors. Commander Farmer, I want full battle readiness within 15 seconds of my orders." Turning back to the view screen without waiting for a response, he found, as he had expected, Phillip D'Amato on the holo.

"Phillip, have your fighters primed and ready. I want an alert cyber squadron ready to go on a moments notice. And just in case, have another on alert 5, will you Phillip?"

He cut off the screen even as the "Aye Sir" came over the comm.

Now came the part all military people hated the most, waiting.

# CHAPTER 4

The DES Stephen Hawking spent seven hours in the descent into the system with all sensors on full and personnel examining every detail of the data available. Upon arrival into the system proper she moved to the location of the destroyed space habitat. Once there her sensors began investigating the destroyed space station/habitat and the colony on the planet or, more accurately, what was left of the space support station and the colony on the planet.

In her engine room, three individuals traded insults and shared work the rest of the crew would not have considered worthy of their degrees or intellect.

"Look," stated Chief Engineer John Roberts, "the Captain wanted to be here in five hours. It took seven. If the stellar engines are not up to the 100% mark, I want the problem fixed. Admiral Price is not a nice man. He will not settle for second best, even from a science ship on the day of his daughter's wedding, and last I heard he was not even married, let alone had a daughter."

"Last I heard," said engineer 2nd class Mike Hotchkins, "he was a bastard and so were all of his children." Laughs filled the engine room at the joke on the admiral's attributes.

"Oh," came the tart response from Roberts, "such a smart attitude, Mr. Hotchkins. You have just earned yourself a trip to the aft manifolds to inspect the injectors."

Hotchkins groaned audibly. The aft manifolds were "combustion chambers" where the fuel was injected and burned for the fusion-powered stellar drive. An airless, filthy, and cramped environment no one wanted to visit on purpose.

On the bridge of the Hawking, various scientists scrutinized the incoming data from her sensors. "It looks like the terraformers were way ahead of schedule. Oxygen levels are adequate but nitrogen is somewhat high. Nothing serious, but I would not want to live in it for extended periods." announced 1st officer Abe Mathews. "Gravity is 1.21 standard gravities. They sure lucked out there."

"Yes, yes. But what was used to destroy the colony? What type of weapons?" inquired Captain Leonard, "You know the Admiral will demand that type of information first."

"Captain," responded his first officer indignantly, "until we know the basics about the planet, I cannot guarantee the accuracy of that answer. But at present, it looks like a combination of clean fusion bombs and some sort of particle ray laser."

"Combination fusion bombs and lasers? They must have been damn small fusion bombs," remarked the Captain.

Abe Matthews may have been the ship's First Officer, but he was a scientist first and foremost, and science was his first love. He had always resented being promoted and having to deal with the day to day routine of running a ship instead of the pure ecstasy of scientific pursuits.

"Captain," came Mathews' irritable response, "they were small highly-focused in their target area and intended to destroy only the general zone or sector. All the bombs destroyed were planetary defense stations. It looks like whomever or whatever did this, plans to use or exploit whatever technology is left. Most of the people and area were exposed to high intensity particle beams. At least," he amended, "that seems to be the case."

"In other words," responded captain Leonard, "they intend to return." Oh shit, oh dear, he thought, the admiral is going to love hearing this kind of news. "Well," he said somewhat reluctantly, "it looks like we have something 'relevant' to report to Admiral Price."

While the Hawking moved in system to inspect the colony and supporting space station, Admiral Price moved the Bismarck and the Nimitz into orbits around two of the planet's four moons. There they remained fairly well hidden.

Aboard the Nimitz, a grim-faced Admiral Price had received the news about the colony. "Captain Leonard," Price rumbled, "continue your investigation. I need all available data on what we are facing."

"And one more thing Captain, a question for your First Officer." Price paused as if gauging his next words carefully. "Considering the nature of the equipment left unattended, what kind of estimate can you give me on the time between destruction of the planetary population and return of whomever or whatever caused the destruction?"

"Excuse me? Admiral, I couldn't *possibly* tell you that. There is weather, type of equipment, and any number of other factors up to and including . . ."

"Commander Matthews!" Price interrupted by way of a bellow. "I am not asking for an exact figure!" Taking a deep breath and quietly cursing scientists and thinkers alike, he summoned up his calmest tones and tried again. "Please, just give me your best estimate."

Looking thoughtful, Matthews drifted into a reverie of blissful scientific pursuit. Just as Admiral Price was beginning to think Matthews had forgotten he was still on screen waiting for a response, it came.

"Sir, most of the equipment would last for several years of exposure. Colony worlds are a strange mixture of medieval tools and top of the line technologies. Most of the high-tech equipment could not last more than about six months without maintenance. It seems to me that those would be the things most valuable to an alien race not familiar with our technology."

"Which means?" asked Price.

"Which means, Sir, that my 'best guess' would be between two and six months, providing of course that they are interested in our high-tech equipment."

"And it has been nearly four months since the original message was sent from the colony regarding the attack." Price mumbled something under his breath then, "Thank you, Captain. Price out."

Mike Hotchkins struggled into his space suit with the help of his friend Anuk.

Anuk was a short, squat, and extremely stout man of Eskimo heritage. While all of his commanders knew his full name, to anyone not in command he was just "Anuk." A good man to have at your back in a bar fight, or at your side in an engine room. His seemingly effortless and endless knowledge of the ebb and flow of power to and from the engines made him an invaluable member of the engineering staff. His strength and girth invaluable in a bar fight.

"Damn Roberts," grumbled Hotchkins. "He has it in for me. Every time there is a lousy job to be done, he sends me."

"Perhaps you should curb your tongue my friend," Anuk stated placidly. "After all, you always seem to have a smart retort for him to hear which, if I may point out, is when he comes up with the 'lousy job' for you to do. This has also benefited you with two rank reductions and one pay reduction."

"Yeah. Right. Thanks for reminding me. I almost forgot about those for a minute. Check the straps on my air bottle, will you?"

"Hotch, you only have three hours of air left in this bottle. We need to swap it out for a fresh one."

"Naw, it's just fine. Shouldn't take more than an hour for the inspection. Besides, I want to get out there and be done as soon as possible so I can get out of this stinking suit."

"May I remind you my friend, that regulations require you to take a full bottle. And since, as you pointed out, Roberts has it 'in for you,' if he finds out that you broke the regs and did not take a full bottle, he will most likely find another 'lousy job' for you to do."

"Also, you cannot afford to get busted. I am telling you my friend, Roberts is ready to bring you before the Captain again."

"All right, all right. Swap it out. But there is no way in hell I am going to stay in this stinking suit for eight hours. Not even three."

The DES Stephen Hawking was now in close orbit to the planet. On the bridge of the Hawking, scientists were busy analyzing data and attempting to piece together the mystery of the attack when all hell broke loose.

"Captain!" came First Mate Baumgardner's excited voice. "We have a normal space incursion happening!"

"What?" Leonard asked, "Where?"

"Fifty thousand klicks off the starboard bow."

"Oh, my God! That is dangerously close. No one in their right mind would re-enter normal space that close to a planet."

"Nevertheless Sir, it is confirmed."

"Sir, Admiral Price on Comm for you," came the excited voice of the communications officer.

"Put him on Mr. Crow."

Price looked and sounded grim as he said, "Captain Leonard, it seems your estimate was more accurate than you would have admitted. We have detected a normal space incursion near your position."

"Yes, Sir. We have detected it as well. I request that you come to our protection with all due haste."

"Negative on that. Until we know more the Nimitz and the Bismarck will remain where they are." Price turned his attention briefly to flip a switch. "Admiral Price to all ships: go to red alert status. Battle stations! This is not a drill!" Turning back to the screen he continued, "Captain Leonard, we can have cyber-fighters to your position in approximately seven minutes. You will stay where you are, monitor the incursion and record all data on the intruder. You will take no provocative action against the intruder until and unless fired upon first. Maintain strict radio silence. Our best ace in the hole may be that they do not know of the presence of the Nimitz and the Bismarck, Price out." With that the channel went dead.

"Sir!" Baumgardner's shocked voice reported, "There are three ships in a tight formation coming through the incursion into normal space."

"Three? Are you sure?"

"Yes, sir. And by their size, all three are capital ships."

"Dear God," Leonard said to himself. "Their Null space technology is incredible! Three capital ships in one tight formation and coming in so close to a planet."

In the Hawking's engine room the klaxon began wailing and the command came over the comm, "Admiral Price to all ships: go to red alert status. Battle stations! This is not a drill!"

Chief engineer Roberts readied the engine room for battle. "Lock down all airtight doors! All reactors to full power! Someone get on the circuit and get Hotchkins back in here now!"

A chorus of "Yes, sir!" resounded. As the other tasks were carried out, Anuk called Hotchkins on the closed circuit. He found, not surprisingly, that Hotchkins had shut off his communications link.

Anuk made a quick decision regarding his friend. Now it appeared that if they survived this encounter, Roberts would find lousy jobs for both of them.

# CHAPTER 5

The holo tank in Chok's cabin lit up and began to chime quietly. Chok deliberately waited for three-tenths of a chron click before answering. "Yes?" Chok did his best to sound bored.

"Chok, this is Admiral Rentahs. Please report to the bridge. We are about to make the incursion into normal space."

"Thank you, Admiral. I will be there as soon as I am finished here."

"Chok, this is Admiral Rentahs. Please report to the bridge. We are about to make the incursion into normal space."

"Flintchiva!" Chok raged as it slammed the off switch to the holo tank, "A recorded message! Of all the insulting . . . gender dominated . . . half eaten feces!" Insult or not, Chok was aware that anger now would be counter-productive. Vowing to return the insult to the Admiral at a later time, Chok somehow managed to rein in its anger and proceed to the bridge.

The bridge of the Ttiflan was bustling with activity. All stations were preparing for the incursion into normal space. From his command chair, Admiral Rentahs supervised the process.

"Science, as soon as we re-enter normal space, I want a complete sensor sweep of the system. Special attention to the fourth planet. Report anything out of the ordinary immediately. Conn, after the incursion, I want a one gravity acceleration to the orbit of the fourth planet."

The door to the aft lift opened and Chok slid onto the bridge. Rentahs did not need to turn to see who it was. All duty officers were already on the bridge. But, even more revealing was that even with the excellent environmental controls on the bridge, there was always an unmistakable stench about a carrion eater like the Binqk. The Admiral noted that he was not the only one who had to swallow several times to keep from losing his gorge.

"Admiral, I must protest," Chok started in.

"Chok! You are on the bridge of *my* ship. You must do nothing but observe. If you cannot do that quietly, then return to your cabin. I am entirely too busy to deal with your nonsense right now."

"Admiral," the conn officer reported, "we have re-entered normal space and are verifying our location now. Location verified, we are in the system Psht Phas Five. Making one gravity acceleration, approaching the fourth planet."

"Admiral!" This from science officer Skarl, "there is a ship in a low orbit around the fourth planet. It does not conform to any known technology."

"Put it on the holo tank Skarl."

"Admiral Rentahs to all ships: Stand at ready alert, but do not take any provocative action. I repeat, no provocative action. Rentahs out."

"What!" demanded Chok, "You must attack immediately. These are the beings that were poisoning our atmosphere! Ready all weapons to fire immediately!"

"Chok!" Rentahs flared angrily. "You do not give orders on my ship! We are not here to further your little war. You are here as an observer. One more outburst like that on my bridge and you will find yourself floating home without so much as an environmental suit. Do we understand each other?"

Chok flushed violet with rage, but said nothing. This was not the time to take action. But the time would come soon enough. And when that time came, Chok vowed to make Rentahs pay dearly for his insults.

Anuk had shrugged into his space suit as quickly as anyone possibly could. Checking the last seal, he made for the access tube leading to the aft manifolds. Without conscious thought, he leaped into the tube to get his friend.

On the bridge of the Hawking, Captain Leonard was busy trying to deal with the overall shock of discovering an intelligent alien race. While simultaneously he fought an internal battle between his desire to go to a science station to observe these alien ships, and the urge to make a run for the third moon and the protection of the Nimitz and the Bismarck.

"All sensors scan those three ships. I want every scrap of data possible. Anything at all could be useful, but until we know more we cannot decide what is and is not useful, so scan and record *everything*."

"Captain!" Abe Matthews said, "We are being scanned. Unusual scans, but scans."

"What do you mean 'unusual' Abe?"

"Unusual to us would be more appropriate. They are scanning our heat signature radiation output and such. Nothing invasive. But I do not recognize the type of scanning beam they are using. And Captain, they are moving toward our position. Slowly, but still approaching us."

"Well, we cannot expect them to not take a look at us."

"Sir," Matthews continued, "if this is the alien race that destroyed the colony and space-based station, we should be battle ready."

"Actually, I couldn't agree more, Abe. However, we are under strict orders to take no provocative action unless fired upon. And, if that was not enough, one science ship against three war ships would not make for much of a fight, more like a slaughter. No, we will wait and see what happens." Then offering his first officer a sly grin, "By the way Abe, I don't see how you figure that this might *not* be the alien race that destroyed the colony. After all, how many alien races can there be?"

Aboard the Flagship Ttiflan of the Fombe fleet, the entire bridge crew was absorbed in their jobs and observing this new alien vessel.

"Admiral," Skarl reported, "the alien ship is in a geosynchronous orbit. There seems to be the remains of a colony of some sort on the planet beneath them, as well as large quantities of debris in a geosynchronous orbit that could have been a station of some sort."

"Very good. Conn, bring us gently and slowly into a geosynchronous orbit, twenty-five percent planetary orbital distance ahead of them."

"Ahead of them sir? We would be sitting ducks to enemy fire!"

"May I remind you madam," Rentahs said stiffly, "that this is not a war zone, nor do we want to make it into one." Relaxing a bit, the Admiral continued, "Besides, we are three cruisers. They are one small ship, indeterminate of power and weaponry true. But somehow I hardly think that this one small ship could pose much of a threat to three cruisers."

"I stand corrected, Sir. Warmth to your bed."

Pleased at the comforting response, Rentahs dropped the matter.

"Communications, stand ready to transmit a standard new race greeting. After all, we want to make friends of these beings."

During this flurry of activity, no one paid any attention to Chok as it casually slid over to an access panel. Palming a device kept hidden within its case coverings, Chok leaned onto the panel, placing the device into direct contact.

On the Nimitz, Admiral Christopher Price was nervous. "Any signs that we have been detected?"

"Negative Sir," responded Science Officer Powell.

"Good. Let's hope it stays that way for now."

"They are, however," continued Powell, "making orbit just ahead of the Hawking. No aggressive overtures yet, Sir."

"Excellent. Communications get me the Bismarck."

"Sir." Captain Heimler stated simply when the channel opened.

"We are in the thick of it now, Vaugn. Is the Bismarck ready?"

"Yes, Sir. We are running silent, but can be at full battle readiness in less than a minute. We await only your orders, Sir."

"Let us hope, Vaugn, that I never need give those orders. Price out."

Aboard the Ttiflan, Admiral Rentahs was making preparations. Unknown to the admiral though, another being was also making preparations. A being with far less peaceful intentions than Admiral Rentahs. "Science report," Rentahs requested.

"Sir. We have been in orbit ahead of the alien ship for nearly a full chron click. They have taken no provocative action. We have been scanned, but . . ."

"Go on," Rentahs urged.

"Sir, they seem to just be observing us. More curious than anything else."

"Have you been able to determine where their bridge is?"

"We believe so, Sir."

"Transfer the coordinates to the communications officer. Comm officer, once you have the coordinates of their bridge, send them a standard new race greeting."

On the bridge of the Hawking, warning lights flared and flashed while the klaxons began sounding.

"Captain! One of the alien ships has just fired an x-ray laser at us!"

"What? Conn take us out of orbit. Make for the Nimitz. Dear God!"

"Sir, wait!" Matthews called. "It is a very low power laser. I cannot believe it is meant to do any harm."

"Just the same Abe, I want to get the hell out of the way if you don't mind! Conn, ahead one full G acceleration. Bring us to point five stellar velocity. And someone, shut off those damn klaxons."

Mike Hotchkins was just finishing up the last minor adjustments to the injectors when suddenly, the engines fired and the accompanying acceleration sent him tumbling and banging his way even further aft in the Jeffries tube. He reached the end of the tube and slammed into the bulkhead hard enough to knock the wind out of him. He reached out for the ladder to right himself and climb back "up" when something large slammed into him hard enough to knock the wind out of him again. There was a distinct snap inside of his suit as his left arm broke under the impact. The great weight on him began to move around and climb off of him. A gloved hand reached around to activate his suit-to-suit communications unit.

"Hi, Hotch. Miss me?" came the voice of Anuk through the comm link.

Aboard the Ttiflan, Admiral Rentahs waited with nominal patience to see what reception the greeting they sent would get from the aliens.

"Admiral," reported Skarl, "the alien has broken orbit and is headed away from our position at a relatively high acceleration."

"Any sign of weapons activity Skarl?"

"Negative Sir."

"Are they running? Or could they be moving to a point where they can get better communications with us?"

"They do not seem to be running, just moving away quickly. The energy signature from their stellar drive seems to be well below what I believe would be safe."

"Very well. Conn, bring the fleet to a parallel, repeat parallel, course. I do not want them to mistake this for a pursuit."

Aboard the Nimitz, a grim faced Admiral Price listened intently to the tight beam transmission from Captain Leonard on the Hawking.

"They have fired an x-ray laser at us. We are heading for your position near the third moon. They are paralleling us at," a quick instrument check, "roughly five hundred thousand kilometers distant. I must repeat my request that the Nimitz and Bismarck come to our aid with all due haste."

"Negative, Captain. Until we know more I do not wish to reveal our position or strengths. You may take any defensive measures you feel necessary, but you are to take no, I repeat no, aggressive action unless attacked."

"Admiral, how do you define an 'attack' if not the firing of an x-ray laser at us?"

"Captain Leonard, you yourself have informed me that no one on your ship has suffered any ill affects from the laser, that it was of a low power. According to your own First Officer, it was not meant to cause harm. At this point, I cannot and will not just assume that this was an attack. I will send a cyber squadron to meet you just in case, but I must reiterate, you will not take any aggressive action. And Captain Leonard, good luck to you Sir. Price out." Turning, he said, "Comm, get me Mr. D'Amato."

Flight Chief Phillip D'Amato answered the Admiral's call almost immediately. "Yes Admiral?"

"Phillip, I want a full cyber squadron launched immediately. They are to rendezvous with the Hawking and provide protection for her as soon as possible. But, they are to take no aggressive action unless an aggressive act is observed. Price out."

"OK ladies," D'Amato said to his cyber pilots, "the Admiral wants a full squadron sent to the Hawking. Let's rock and roll."

Cyber pilots are a breed apart from regular fighter pilots. Most were women for one thing. Women seemed better able to keep track of the numerous details necessary to fly at tremendous speeds and pull the types of maneuvers only cyberfighters could manage. But more importantly, cyber pilots never entered their planes. They "flew" up to five fighters at once, by plugging their cybernetic implants directly into the control panel aboard the mothership. This eliminated the need for mechanical controls and cut down on response time. Not being physically in their fighters enabled them to perform maneuvers with G-forces well in excess of what a manned ship could do. In short, they could accelerate faster, turn sharper, respond quicker, and have more power for weaponry, because their ships did not have to provide life support or worry about killing a pilot.

Another advantage was that a two-person fighter could have one fighter jock and one rear and a wingman with the same compliment. The cyber pilot, while controlling up to five cyberfighters, virtually eliminated the need for a wingman. The cyber pilot might even use one of the cyberfighters to ram incoming ships or missiles, if their defensive weapons could not be brought to bear quickly enough.

In fact, the only disadvantages realized by the military minds of Earth and her colonies was that there were so very few people capable of becoming cyber pilots. Maybe, one in seventy thousand. That, and the range restrictions from the mothership. At one full AU, there was a .73-second time lag. Not much really, unless your vessel is flying at .5 C. Then, it could get rather dicey.

At D'Amato's orders, five cyber pilots plugged in, did pre-flight checks, and launched twenty-five cyberfighters in less than two minutes. From there, they accelerated toward the Hawking at nearly one hundred gravities.

# CHAPTER 6

Aboard the Ttiflan, Admiral Rentahs was growing moody.

"Comm, still no response to our message?"

"No response, Admiral. It is within the realm of possibility that they did not get clear reception. And, as you suggested earlier, might be moving to a better reception point."

"Admiral Rentahs," Chok interjected smoothly, "perhaps you should send your message again?"

Rentahs considered berating Chok for interfering, but decided against it. After all, it was a reasonable suggestion. So instead he merely turned to his communications officer and said, "Comm, send the message again."

Chok showed no outward changes, but rewarded itself with a burst of endorphin. This was the opportunity it had waited for.

As the communications officer started re-sending the standard new race greeting, Chok reached into its coverings and flipped a switch on a remote control device.

"Admiral Rentahs!" the communications officer yelled, "Our greeting transmission . . ."

"Yes, what is it?"

"Somehow the power output from the communications laser just increased nearly one thousand percent!"

"What? How? Never mind that now. Shut it down. Shut it down immediately!"

"I am trying Sir, but I seem to have no control over the comm system. Control seems to have been re-routed to somewhere else."

"Cold empty bed." muttered Rentahs. "What have we done?"

On board the Hawking, Abe Matthews was monitoring the alien ship's paralleling them and reviewing the scanner information, when the warning lights started flaring and the klaxons began wailing again.

"Report!" demanded Leonard.

"Captain, they are shooting another of those low power x-ray lasers directly at our bridge."

"At the bridge? Are you sure about that Abe?"

"Yes Sir, one moment." Nearly ten seconds went by while the captain waited and sweated "Randolph! Prime numbers! It's a message! They are transmitting prime numbers and mathematical constants via the x-ray laser."

"My God!" came Leonard's relieved response. "Make sure you get a recording. Use however much computer power and time necessary to give us a working language.

"Communications get me Admiral Price. This is wonderful news. The Admiral . . ."

Sudden waves of nausea swept over Captain Leonard. His entire body seemed to go limp and he had no control of it anymore. He collapsed onto the deck. His bladder and bowels both emptied themselves. His mind sluggishly tried to figure out what was happening. He was vaguely aware that the rest of the bridge crew had collapsed and befouled themselves as well. His normally focused mind could not seem to keep a thought straight. The lighting went out and all the bridge equipment shut down. It was dark, the kind of dark normally reserved for underground caves. Not even one small star in the distance for light. Something else was also wrong, something that seemed to demand the captain's notice. Captain Leonard fought to focus his mind on the issue, to figure out what it was. He was mildly pleased with himself when he realized what the problem was. There was no hum from the environmental systems. They would all suffocate soon, if nothing was done.

It was the last thought Captain Randolph Leonard would ever have.

# CHAPTER 7

"Cyber One to Admiral Price."

"Price. Go ahead Cyber One."

"Sir, the alien fleet has just fired another x-ray laser at the Hawking. I now believe the low power beam was merely a target acquisition beam. Sir, this time, the low power shot tracked to the Hawking's bridge, then its power level shot off the scale, way beyond the capabilities of my instruments to measure. The Hawking appears dead in space. Your orders sir?"

"One moment Cyber One." Turning, Price barked simply, "Science? Can you confirm?"

"Checking Admiral," the suddenly white-faced ensign at science said. His hands shook visibly while he checked his instruments. "Sir, the Hawking appears dead in space. No electromagnetic output. Stellar drive seems to be in complete shutdown mode. I would have to say that she is dead, Sir."

Admiral Christopher Price said nothing. The only clue that he had heard his science officer was when he slammed his fist down hard on the arm of his command chair.

"Cyber One this is Admiral Price. Continue on course to the Hawking. Protect that ship. I repeat, protect that ship. You will take whatever steps are necessary to keep that ship out of the hands of the aliens. Price out.

"Communications get me the Bismarck. I want to speak to Captain Hiemler immediately. I don't care if he is sitting on the head have his comm officer run a line. Then get me Flight Chief D'Amato again."

Toggling a switch, he made the announcement: "Battle stations! All hands to battle stations! This is not a drill! The Hawking has been destroyed by enemy fire. All hands to battle stations!"

On the bridge of the Ttiflan, Admiral Rentahs was furious.

"The alien ship appears to be dead, Admiral," Skarl informed him. "No energy signature, no electromagnetic output, and the stellar drive has completely shut down."

"Admiral Rentahs! We have found where the communication systems have been re-routed to. It is routed to a device in Special Representative Chok's quarters, via a device attached to one of our access panels. And Sir," continued the communications officer, "both of the devices are definitely of Binqk origin."

"Master at Arms," the Admiral said with a deadly calm. "Arrest Special Representative Chok immediately. I want Chok, and then its quarters, strip—searched. And confine Chok to the brig.

The Master at Arms obeyed her orders unquestioningly, while Chok raged.

"This is an outrage! I am a Special Representative of the Binqk empire! I am here on the orders of the Galactic Council. You have no right to treat me in this manner!"

"Silence!" bellowed Rentahs. "You are on a Fombe ship, not a Binqk ship. According to our laws, you have committed acts of both sabotage and treason. I would disembowel you myself right here and now were it not for your foul stench and the insult it would cause to my officers. Master at Arms, you have your orders. If it so much as annoys you . . ."

"Admiral," Skarl interrupted urgently, "I have detected twenty-five objects under power heading toward our position."

"Objects, Skarl? Can you be a little more specific?"

"Sir, they are too large and complex to be missiles, and yet too small to be ships. They are coming on a direct course for the alien ship at an impossibly high acceleration."

"Shoot them!" screamed Chok. "Shoot them now!"

"Master at Arms, silence that—creature—and remove it from my bridge," Rentahs ordered. "Search it thoroughly and confine it to the brig. If it offers any resistance, any at all, you have my authority to use any amount of force you see fit. Up to and including deadly force. Captain Pomb, please make a special note of that in the ship's log."

"Admiral," Captain Pomb spoke up, "warmth to your bed, Sir. I know that I am still in admiralty training and it is therefore not my place to speak. But, considering the nature of the events that just occurred, I think we must assume that these objects are not mere probes, but some form of weapons. Should we not take defensive measures immediately, certainly against these probable weapons and against the ship or ships that launched them, Sir?"

"Ship or ships that launched them?" Rentahs inquired.

"Sir, they are obviously too small to have traveled to this system on their own. They had to be brought here by a mothership of some sort. May I suggest we look near the moons as they seemed to have come from that general section of space.

"Well thought out and stated, Captain Pomb. As well as correct. You may bring the fleet to battle readiness. Communications get the commanders of the Catchiflan and the Xyflan. We have another problem to solve before those devices get here—if we have the time," Rentahs worried aloud.

In the Jeffries tube at the aft manifold of the Hawking, Anuk was helping Hotchkins up the ladder to the engine room when the lighting suddenly went out and the acceleration ceased. With the sudden lack of acceleration, the two men found themselves weightless and propelled forward by their own efforts, losing their grips on the ladder and causing them to slam into a bulkhead.

Mike Hotchkins temper got the best of him. "Shit! What the hell does that asshole Leonard think he is doing up there?"

"Wait Hotch," Anuk said calmly but with great seriousness, "something is wrong. Terribly wrong."

"More of your Eskimo Wisdom, Anuk? Let me guess. An otter told you. Or was it a bear?"

"Hotch, feel the ship. No vibrations."

Hotchkins had been aboard ships long enough to know that even when powered down there was always some vibration. Even if only the environmental controls were functioning, the circulation fans caused minute vibrations throughout the ship. But this ship was dead. Suddenly, Mike Hotchkins felt very cold inside. "We had better get to the engine room, Anuk. Something tells me we are in serious trouble."

Mike Hotchkins could not see the grin on his friend's face as Anuk retorted, "More of your White Man wisdom, Hotch? Let me guess. An angel told you. Or was it a leprechaun?"

"Cyber One, please tie me in directly to Admiral Price."

"Go ahead Cyber One."

"Admiral, two of the alien ships are moving to intercept us. The third is moving to close proximity of the Hawking and appears to be launching a shuttle of some sort. Should we engage the lone ship or the two?"

"Neither, Cyber One. Scrap that shuttle. I say again, scrap the shuttle. Then proceed at your discretion. The Nimitz and Bismarck are less than two hours behind you and a second cyber squadron is on its way. E.T.A. to you is seven minutes. If you can keep them busy until we get there, we can take out those big boys for you, providing you don't take them out before we get there. Price out."

Aboard the shuttle, Flanpodin, the security team was readying themselves for a search and rescue. "Search for survivors and rescue them. Search for some kind of map or mapping system and retrieve that as well," had been the Admiral's orders.

After locating what appeared to be an airlock near the bridge, they made their way onto the dead ship and into a darkness that seemed to swallow the light from their hand torches.

In the engine room of the Hawking, two lone figures were looking around with the help of their suit lights. The pervading darkness made the grim sight of comrades fallen, without any sign of struggle or retaliation, all the more gruesome.

"I think I'm gonna puke," said Hotchkins.

"Be sure you remove your helmet first," Anuk stated, "we may have to keep these suits on for a while once the air in the ship becomes unbreathable. And, it would be most unfortunate if you had to share your suit with this morning's breakfast."

"Thanks, Anuk. That was a visual image I could have lived without. Any ideas about what killed them? Or why it didn't kill us?"

"Several ideas on what killed them—none I would swear by. But from the look of things, the only reason we are still alive is that the shielding around the manifolds protected us from whatever weapon they used. Give me a hand here."

The two men grabbed a body that lay sprawled over an instrument console and moved it out of the way.

"You know," Hotchkins said offhandedly, "I've always wanted to tell Roberts he was full of shit. But from the mess he made of this console and his trousers, even I had no idea how true that was."

"Give the man a break," said Anuk, "he is dead, after all."

"I was just thinking that I've never seen Roberts look more lifelike."

"I get no readings from any of these instruments. They should be working, though." Anuk opened up the back of the console and peered inside. "Fused, every circuit burned out. If this happened to the entire ship, this is nothing but a floating hulk. Let's get up to the bridge and see if anyone is alive up there."

Just as they unlatched the airtight door to leave the engine room, the door swung open seemingly of its own volition. Eight figures in unfamiliar space suits entered. Anuk quickly backed away, but two of them grabbed Hotchkins and held him.

The other six came after Anuk. As he backed away, Anuk took a quick look around and grabbed the first thing he could use as an improvised weapon. A forty millimeter spanner.

On the Bridge of the Nimitz, Admiral Christopher Price was getting yet another report from Cyber One.

"The two lead ships each launched a missile which when detonated turned out to be electromagnetic pulse bombs approximately eight hundred and fifty kilometers in front of our fighters. We barely had time to pull up and avoid the pulse. It would have fried every power component on the ships, but would not have harmed a living pilot."

"So this tactic was meant to delay, not destroy your ships. Is that what you are suggesting?" inquired the Admiral.

"I believe that is the case, Sir. It will take us an extra five to seven minutes to go around. But Sir, their shuttle is already docked with the Hawking."

"I see. Your orders still stand. Take whatever measures are necessary to keep the Hawking and anything taken from her out of the hands of the aliens. Scrap that shuttle. I repeat, scrap the shuttle. I want nothing taken from the Hawking to reach that capital ship. Price out."

Anuk found himself being half-carried and half-pushed by three of the aliens into the airlock where the alien shuttle was docked. Once inside the airlock, he took a good look at the aliens in their strange space suits. They were bipedal with two arms averaging just over seven feet tall. In fact, was it not for the strange design of the suits and the fact that they apparently had an extra joint in both arms and legs, he might have mistaken them for extremely tall humans.

One of the aliens shoved the helmet from Anuk's own space suit into his hands and made gestures for Anuk to put it on. As he placed his suit helmet on his head and fastened the seals, one of the aliens entered the lock carrying two air bottles for space suits. Setting them down it turned, shut and latched the airlock, then proceeded to cycle the air.

Once aboard the alien shuttle, the aliens removed their own helmets and Anuk got his first real look at them. Their skin was a ruddy brown, the tops and sides of their heads covered with purple hair-like cilia. Three eyes, a larger one in the middle of their "forehead" the other two farther apart than human eyes, though obviously used for binocular vision. No nose, but a single hole where a nose would be on a human. A mouth similar to a human mouth, apparently it had very thin lips and was located in the same place on their heads as a human mouth would be.

Further observation would have to be delayed as he was ushered to a "cabin" on the shuttle where he found a familiar face in a space suit. Mike Hotchkins spoke on the suit-to-suit radio.

"Anuk! God, I thought they were going to kill you when you put up a fight. But I sure am glad to see your ugly face."

"It is good to see you too my friend, though I have no idea for how long we will be together."

"What do you mean?" inquired Hotchkins. "Do you have reason to think they might separate us?"

"Simply put my friend, we are definitely prisoners, so we have little or no control over what they do with us. Further, we do not know if we are merely prisoners of war, or dinner to these people."

With a loud clanking sound, the shuttle shook slightly and then there was a feeling of "gravity" indicating acceleration.

Looking around, Anuk made note that there was one padded bench or bed against the bulkhead that was "down" to the acceleration of the vessel.

"We had better make use of the bench, Hotch. I have a feeling we may need some padding for upcoming acceleration."

No sooner had the pair sat on the bench when, a loud klaxon started sounding and the acceleration increased dramatically. Three rapid explosions rocked the shuttle violently. Both Anuk and Hotchkins were thrown from the bench to the deck, only to be slammed back "down" against the bulkhead again as the acceleration increased once more.

Anuk found himself unable to move from the bulkhead pinned as it were, by the acceleration. Unable to see his friend's face, but able to tell Hotch was lying on his broken arm, he attempted to check on Hotch via the suit-to-suit radio. There was no response.

Another explosion, this one seemingly right inside the cabin containing the two humans. Anuk was dizzy, the cabin seemed to spin around as if he had imbibed too much "rocket juice." Things started to get darker and the final thought that ran through his addled brain was "is Hotchkins still alive?"

On the bridge of the Ttiflan, Admiral Rentahs was trying to make sense of what was happening.

"Admiral, I read two capital ships coming our way. They appear to have been hiding behind two of the moons, Sir."

"Understood. Skarl can you tell me what those other objects are yet?"

"Negative, sir. They skirted around the electromagnetic pulse bomb's periphery as if they were manned by an intelligence. They appear to have all the attributes of a small fighter craft, yet there appears no room aboard them for carrying a pilot. At present, they have circumvented the electromagnetic pulse and are headed directly for either the Flanpodin or possibly the alien ship—it is difficult to say which yet. But the Flanpodin has departed the alien ship and is now headed back to the Ttiflan."

"Admiral," reported the communications officer, "the Flanpodin reports it has captured two of the aliens from the their ship. No other survivors."

"Did they recover any form of mapping system?"

"Unknown sir. They did say all of the navigational equipment seemed to be computerized and that all electronic components seem to have been ruined by our x-ray laser."

"Admiral," Skarl reported, "the alien objects are converging on the Flanpodin, and the lead object is opening fire."

"Cold bed! Opening fire? Without a pilot? I do not understand how this could be, but I do know we need those survivors if we are to have any chance of stopping this war before it goes any further than this meeting. Skarl, are you quite certain those objects are unoccupied?"

"I cannot say for absolute certain, Sir, but from what we have been able to extrapolate of the size of these aliens, there is no way one of them could be on board one of those objects—though I do not understand how they could fly and fight the way they do without a pilot."

"Very well." Toggling a switch, Admiral Rentahs made a ship-wide announcement, "All batteries open up on the alien objects attacking our shuttle. Fire at will. I repeat, fire at will."

On the shuttle Flanpodin, the pilot realized she was in serious trouble. The alien objects had already scored four shots on them and their defensive systems were down. The Ttiflan had returned fire, but with mixed success. Her lasers and particle beams seemed to have little or no effect. The tiny alien ships—she decided she might as well call them ships—dodged and danced in and out of the lasers and particle beams in unbelievably intricate high G exercises. No Fombe could have survived those maneuvers, but their missiles could and did keep up with the gambit. Eleven of the alien ships had flared up into incandescent dust, though the aliens had shown a great deal of skill at anti-missile technology.

But, she still had to find a way to get back aboard the Ttiflan without the remainder of the alien ships destroying her already crippled shuttle.

Making a quick and dangerous choice, she accelerated to maximum safe G force plus ten percent. The Flanpodin raced to the Ttiflan's shuttle bay, her braking thrusters not firing until she passed the entrance. "Too late," she sighed, as another alien missile slammed into the shuttle and the resulting explosion slammed the small ship onto the deck with a bone crunching crash. There, she skidded out of control for one hundred meters before crashing into another shuttle, rolling onto its side, and then crashing into the bulkhead at the far end of the deck.

Under the weight of a three-G acceleration, Admiral Price was pressed back into his command chair. His face stretched back to make his normally severe looking face seem almost skeletal. "Cyber One, what is your status?" demanded Price.

"Admiral, we have sustained heavy casualties. My squadron is down to fourteen ships. The alien's missiles have incredibly good tracking and maneuvering capabilities. We were unable to prevent the shuttle from reaching the mothership, but it took heavy damage before it crashed onto the deck. I doubt much of anything could have survived at the speed it was moving when it hit. It also seems to have caused heavy damage to their mothership. The other two capital ships have moved in closer to provide cover for the first. Cyber Two and her squadron are just now entering strike range."

"Damn!" Price said to no one in particular. "Cyber One, you are to use whatever means necessary to destroy that first enemy ship. We have no idea what the aliens might have taken off of the Hawking, and we dare not let them get anything they can use against us later. Price out."

On the bridge of the Ttiflan, Admiral Rentahs was getting a damage assessment and did not like the results.

"Captain Pomb, order the Catchiflan and Xyflan to move into a defensive position between us and the incoming capital ships and launch every available fighter from all of our ships."

"Sir!" Captain Pomb exclaimed, "Our fighters are no match for those alien fighter craft. To send our people out in fighters against those alien ships would be a death sentence."

"I am aware of that, Captain Pomb. It is most unpleasant as well as unfortunate. But, if we are to find a way to stop this war from escalating, we need the information retrieved from the alien ship. Pray that what we need is still intact."

"Inform the captains of the Catchiflan and Xyflan that they are to distract the aliens long enough for us to make a jump. Then, they are to make all efforts to disengage and make a jump for home as fast as possible.

"Conn, take us far enough away from the fighting that we can open an incursion into null space."

"Admiral Price! The alien ships have all launched fighters and are attempting to engage our fighters. And Sir," continued the young ensign at science, "one of their capital ships is leaving the area of the fighting."

"How many fighters have they launched?"

"Approximately sixty sir."

"Admiral?" inquired the Communications Officer, "should I raise Cyber One for you?"

"Negative, Cyber One will be quite occupied just now."

"Admiral, Captain Hiemler for you, Sir."

"Very well. Put him on. Yes Vaugn, what is it?"

"Admiral, I suggest you take the Nimitz after the ship that is running away from the fray. The Bismarck can handle those other two big birds, Sir."

"Excellent suggestion, Vaugn. We will proceed as you have suggested. Good luck. Price out."

Captain Pomb looked ill. It was clear he was distressed as well. Though he never quite crossed the line to insubordination, he made his feelings about what he had to report completely clear. "Admiral our fighters are keeping the alien fighters occupied as per your orders Sir, by being used for target practice." One of the alien capital ships is engaging both the Catchiflan and the Xyflan. The other is headed directly at us. Your orders, Sir?"

"Continue on course. We need to create an incursion and go home," the Admiral said, ignoring the nearly insubordinate tone and words.

All throughout the Bismarck, men and women had already made preparations for going into battle. Stations were manned, checks made on all equipment, and readiness reported to the section chiefs. Many of those men and women made time after that for a short prayer. The bridge itself was bustling with activity as each department head received readiness reports from section chiefs. Then, the department heads reported readiness to Commander Andreiovich.

Commander Alexi Andreiovich was moving up fast through the ranks of the DES Navy. He was the second youngest person to achieve the rank of Commander in the history of the entire DES Navy and he had full intention of being the youngest to be promoted to captain.

Whip thin, but with unexpected strength from daily workouts in zero gravity environments, he was also a master of two martial arts. The hard lines of his face and strikingly large nose had earned him the nickname "The Hawk" among his former classmates at the academy. Nowadays, they called him "Sir," and saluted.

Alexi reported to the Captain. "All stations report ready, all weapons manned and charged, all reactors up to full power, and emergency repair teams are standing by on all decks and stations."

"Very good Commander," responded Captain Hiemler. "Let's take her in."

"Course sir?" inquired Alexi.

"Zero-two-seven, mark five-five-three, Commander."

"Begging the Captain's pardon," Alexi inquired, "but that course will take us directly between the two alien capital ships. Can we be sure that the Bismarck can take on both of them at one time, Sir?"

"Your concern is noted, Commander. However, you have seen for yourself how well our cyberfighters handled their fighter craft. I think that gives us ample reason to believe the Bismarck can handle their capital ships in the same way."

Alexi shared no such beliefs, but was loath to contradict his captain in front of the crew.

The Bismarck came into firing range but, at her captain's orders, held her fire. She shook with the impact of three missiles—five other alien missiles had been destroyed or disabled before reaching their target. As the battleship came between the two aliens, Captain Hiemler ordered all weapons to fire a double broadside.

The broadsides slammed into the two alien ships. Explosions from her barrage hammered away. Lasers cut holes into their hulls, causing atmosphere to come gushing out in great expanding clouds of gaseous ice. Her surface rail guns threw fifty-ton nickel iron rocks that tore and ripped their way through bulkheads, equipment, and crew quite easily at over 500 KPH. Her cannons were used to take out primary targets like the bridge, communications, sensors, weapons, power transfer points, and engines.

The aliens fired back at the Bismarck. On the bridge, it felt like a great earthquake shaking the entire ship—the deck was pitching and rolling violently. Men and women screamed in pain and terror.

"Report!" demanded the Captain.

"Sir!" Alexi responded. "We have inflicted heavy damage on both alien ships. Our shielding has protected us fairly well from their particle and x-ray weapons.

Not quite as well as we had hoped though. We have sustained heavy damage to our jump engines. There are hull breaches on decks three, seven, eight, nine, eleven, and thirteen; sections alpha through gamma port side and alpha through juliet on the starboard side. We have lost four rail guns, five cannons, three starboard and two port lasers, both starboard. Minor damage to life support systems, but nothing we cannot handle. I have reports of eighty seven dead and as many as one hundred twenty missing."

"Damn! Damn, damn, and double damn! Very well, Alexi," the Captain said, "bring us about to course two-one-eight mark one-one-two. Fire all weapons except the rail guns as they come to bear."

"Aye, aye, Sir."

The Bismarck made a tight turn and returned to pass between the two aliens again. One of the aliens made to move off. The other seemed to have sustained enough damage to her stellar engines that she could not move away.

"Alexi, have all the rail guns target that wounded bird and fire at optimum range."

"Aye, Sir," Alexi responded, passing the command down to the weapons officer.

As the Bismarck moved in for a second salvo, both the aliens opened up with their own barrage. The deck plates screamed their protest as they buckled under the torture of weapons fire. Fire and explosions rocked the bridge and the crew was tossed about like puppets within their safety netting.

Alexi found himself pressed hard into the safety netting that kept him in his control couch. He felt flattened, and could not inhale enough air to scream. The bridge was filling with an acrid smoke from several control consoles that were on fire. People were yelling—some in pain, some in terror, a few requesting orders.

"Captain?" inquired Alexi. Unable to see the command couch through the smoke and getting no response from the captain, Alexi unfastened his safety netting and went to his captain. The captain's command couch had been torn almost completely out of the decking. It lay nearly upside down on the deck. Unable to see his captain, Alexi reached around to check the man's pulse. His hand found a warm, moist pulp where the captain's head and neck used to be.

Retrieving his hand from the grisly mess he issued his own command, "All stations report!"

"One alien ship appears dead in space. The other is disengaging and moving away at low acceleration."

"Hull breaches on all decks except one and fourteen. Repair crews are responding."

"Engine room reports it needs to shut down reactors two and three due to coolant leaks."

"Life support is out. Repair time nearly twenty minutes."

"I have a report that sick bay has been completely destroyed."

"Communications are totally out with the exception of internal ship's communications, sir."

Great. Just great, thought Alexi. Hiemler sure picked a lousy time to get himself killed.

"Science, I want you to keep an eye on the dead alien ship. I don't want to find out the hard way that she is not dead." Almost as an afterthought he added, "and keep a trace on the other ship. If she circles back I want to know before she gets here."

"Aye, aye, Sir. Uh, Commander?" Came the response from the ensign at science, "should I have a medical team report here for the captain?"

"The captain is dead, but we have other injured. Tell them to send one medic for now. Let the medic determine if we need a team here. Though I think you will find there are wounded aboard that have more desperate need of a medical team."

"Communications, is there any way we can raise Admiral Price on the Nimitz?"

"Negative, Sir."

"Understood. I won't ask for an estimate, but get something patched in as soon as possible, then track me down immediately." Turning he continued, "Science, can you tell me what is happening with the Nimitz?"

"I'm sorry, Sir," the young ensign responded, "our sensors were severely damaged. I do not have the capability to keep scans on three things now. Should I stop monitoring one of the aliens, Sir?"

"Absolutely not. Keep track of those aliens. I want no surprises."

Seriously wounded by the alien "fighters, missles?" the Ttiflan struggled to get far enough away from the energy discharges of the battle to make an incursion into null space. The alien vessel was rapidly closing in. Rentahs turned to the science station. "Skarl, will the alien ship get within striking distance before we can jump?"

"It is difficult to say for certain sir. Our stellar engines are damaged and we can barely maintain our present acceleration. But unless they increase their acceleration drastically, I seriously doubt it, Sir."

"Good. Captain Pomb you have the Conn. Make the jump for home as soon as you can. I have one more chore to take care of before we leave this system."

With that, Admiral Rentahs turned to the aft lift and left the bridge. Making his way to the brig he approached the only occupied cell.

"Special Representative Chok of the Binqk Empire. Are you quite comfortable?" the admiral asked sarcastically.

"You will pay for your insolence. This is a complete outrage! The Binqk Empire will require much recompense for your deeds this day."

"Chok, your conduct this day has already cost the lives of more than three hundred of my people on this ship alone. And many more of my people may yet die because of your actions. Not to mention the lives of many of these aliens. You have committed acts of sabotage, treason, and espionage. I have only one duty left to perform before we leave this system."

"And what would that be, Admiral?" Chok sneered.

In answer, Admiral Rentahs reached out and pressed a single button.

One thousand four hundred and seventy years later a Zirtrail mining ship, returning from the asteroid belt, would accidentally discover the desiccated body of Binqk Special Representative Chok, floating in space.

Admiral Price squirmed in his command couch and watched the battle between the Bismarck and the two aliens on the main view screen. Even with three G's of acceleration he could not hold still. He knew that many men and women were dying over there and could not stand the idea that they were dying for no reason. Mentally he urged the Nimitz to move even faster and toyed with the idea of increasing their acceleration. But, with the amount of time they had been at three G's of acceleration, he did not dare. If they got within striking distance of the alien ship, he needed his crew able to fight, not falling down exhausted from the hard acceleration.

Suddenly his science officer barked, "Admiral, the aliens have opened an incursion!"

"Damn!" swore the Admiral. "Launch our fighters. Inform them to shut down the incursion and then worry about the alien ship."

"Sir, our fighters won't have time to reach them before the alien can make the jump."

"Check to see if any of our cyberfighters can make it in time to shut down the incursion. I don't care if they run out of fuel doing so. We have to stop that ship from leaving the system."

"Negative, Sir. Cyber One reports her fighters barely have enough fuel to return to the Nimitz. Some already need to shut down and wait until the Nimitz moves to make rescue as it is."

The admiral used a string of invectives that made some of the newer ensigns on the bridge blush. "Well, whatever they took off the Hawking, they got away with it," Price stated.

"Conn, make course back to the Bismarck and our cyberfighters."

# CHAPTER 8

In the healing chambers of the Ttiflan, the third shift senior physician on duty, Mulci, was ecstatic. "Such a great day for Clan Flan," she thought to herself. "First we undermine the plan of Clan Nakt to disgrace us with a mission involving the Binqk by actually discovering a new sapient space-going species. Then we gain even more clan status by becoming the Fombe experts on these humans." A wry smile worked its way onto her face. "Not to mention what becoming the Senior Fombe Physician on Human Biology and Physiology is going to mean to myself. More clan and family status, more social status, rapid advancement within ship's rank, a larger credit rating each month, and bigger quarters!"

Mulci was interrupted from her reverie by her desk chiming softly.

Touching the control to respond she saw her secretary's flushed and grinning face. "Yes, Tiko. I can tell from your expression that it is more bad news. Tell me anyway. I can take it, I'm strong." She joked.

"Mulci! Admiral Rentahs himself has requested you to join him for fourth-shift meal!"

"Really, well I suppose that it should have been expected," she said as flatly as if it was of no consequence. "The admiral would want a report from the senior physician on duty when the humans came in."

"Mulci!" Tiko said accusingly, "don't you get it? Admiral Rentahs wants to see you."

"I understand that. Is there anything else? No? Then thank you, Tiko." With that she shut the connection.

Waiting a few hundredths of a chron click to make sure the connection was closed she jumped out of her seat and let out a loud squeal of delight.

Since Mulci was expected for the fourth-shift meal, and since the custom was to take the meal at the beginning of the shift, Mulci did exactly what Fombe protocol dictated. Precisely at the chime that signaled the beginning of the fourth-shift, she walked into the admiral's private cabin unannounced and sat down at his personal dining table.

She had barely taken her seat when Admiral Rentahs, seated at his desk reading an electronic note pad, finally stood up, stretched and started toward the dining table. Noting that his guest had arrived he simply said, "Ah, Mulci is it not?"

"Yes, Admiral."

"Mailiew. but Maili will do in here, unless you would prefer me to refer to you by your full title: Third Shift Senior Physician Mulci of Clan Flan."

"Cold bed no. I prefer Mulci."

Rentahs took a good look. She seemed middle-aged by Fombe standards. Large, but not fat. She moved like a wild animal. Sleek and graceful, but strong and muscular, it almost seemed she was part feline. Quickly Rentahs pushed that thought away for later.

"Very well, Mulci and Maili it shall be," stated the admiral graciously.

Taking his own seat, Rentahs tapped a device on the table's control panel. A small communications screen slid up and leaned back above the table to make reading easier. On the screen was Admiral Rentahs's personal chef.

"Warmth to your bed, Rentahs. Your preference in food this meal?" asked the chef.

Rentahs asked Mulci for her order, placed both orders with the chef, shut down the communications panel, and turned to Mulci.

"How are our alien guests doing, Mulci?"

"One regained consciousness about two and a tenth chron clicks before your invitation to dinner. He has some bruises, abrasions, and minor scrapes. One minor bone fracture in his right arm, another in his right hand, and one loose tooth." This last was said with a small wicked smile.

"A loose tooth?" Rentahs asked curiously.

"Yes. A loose tooth," Mulci replied trying hard not to laugh. "It seems that after finding his shipmates all dead and our security team marching in grabbing the only other survivor and dragging him out of the room, this fellow put up quite a fight."

Rentahs lifted his left ear curiously. Then, his center eye dilating, his outer two eyes came to focus on Mulci. In Fombe body language he was displaying considerable interest. "Do go on, please. I am finding this to be quite interesting news," he said with just a touch of a smile creeping onto his face.

"Three of our brightest and best security people," she said, "managed to get themselves killed in the search and rescue mission by charging this particular alien and then, in the usual trained and efficient manner displayed by security, they backed him into a corner and tried to physically grab him. Keep in mind that the second most dangerous creature in the known universe is a cornered creature that feels threatened. When our alien picked up an object they didn't recognize, they didn't think twice about it and continued with their attempts to physically grab this fellow.

"Our alien friend then smashed the face plates on two of our security peoples' helmets and broke off the supply valve of another's air supply while they were trying to grab him.

"Two more security people are in my hospital with broken legs, two with broken arms, and another with one of each broken. All of this before some ninny stunned the alien and ruined all of the fun security was having getting themselves maimed and killed."

"Ha!" laughed Rentahs, "I like this fellow already. But you haven't explained the loose tooth."

"I was just getting to that!" Both of them were laughing now. "Once the alien was stunned, he fell with his helmet next to a bulkhead. One of the security boys was so upset about all of the mayhem and three dead partners that he kicked the alien's helmet into the bulkhead This caused the loose tooth when the alien bounced his mouth off the readouts in his helmet."

"I take it you know which of the officers, and on which security team it was?" Rentahs asked very seriously, "Because that officer is going to be demoted for his stupidity."

"Oh, I would not worry about that too much. That officer suffered three broken bones in the offending foot and because of the way the bones happened to break, he will never walk normally again. When the Master at Arms found out what this security officer had done, she informed him exactly how stupid he was, in long sentences punctuated with several curses. There were colorful references to his personal hygiene or lack thereof and his complete inability to breed a child smarter than a support beam. She then stripped him of all rank and seniority, made sure he knew there was no way he would ever get out of the security department, and that he would never move up in rank or seniority.

"Then as an added bonus, the Master at Arms left standing orders that as soon as this former officer is healed enough to 'crawl through muck, that he is to be 'discharged to duty.' Wherein, he then gets to personally search all of the septic systems in the entire ship thoroughly, to make sure that the Binqk we had on board didn't plant a bomb by disposing of it in the septic system."

Rentahs was laughing so hard he nearly fell from his seat. Eventually he regained enough composure to respond. "I should have known the Master at Arms would see to the situation without any help from me."

"All I can say is that I am glad I work in the infirmary and not in security right now," commented Mulci.

"I don't blame you. But what about the other alien?"

"The other is not doing as well as the first. He has a compound fracture in his left arm just below the elbow. Did you know they only have one elbow in each arm and one knee to each leg? No? I mentioned them being bipeds didn't I? No? Well, along with that he has four broken chest support bones. Their chest bones are far more flexible than ours, but not nearly as strong.

He has multiple abrasions and severe bruising including some bruising to internal organs. A very basic organ setup, just different locations though only a single pump for the circulatory system. This is quite peculiar, rare to the Nth degree, and they have one other organ we find no use for and can't seem to figure out. Maybe when we learn some more of their language they can explain it.

"He, did I mention both are males? No? He also took a severe blow to his head. Their brain is located in their head, as is ours—therefore he is presently unconscious—some type of neurological shock from the impact. I don't dare treat him surgically until I know enough about their physiology and biochemistry to program the instruments. My experience with this type of injury in most species suggests that neurological shock of this type is best treated surgically. But if it cannot be treated surgically, then it is best left alone.

"The dermal regenerator worked well, with minor reprogramming of the instrument. I have healed the abrasions and epidermal bruises, though the swelling will take time to go down.

"The broken bones I can repair. Biologically they are not that different from us. However, I need to wait until he is conscious to repair them."

"Why?" interrupted Rentahs, "if they are so biologically close?"

"The other alien is still being treated for his fractures. We found that we could regenerate the bone, but that the patient was unusually sensitive to the treatment. He seemed to be responding perfectly normally at first, but then he became nauseous and made it clear it was causing him physical discomfort. We have since discovered that he can tolerate shorter low intensity bursts if we give him breaks, but our only guideline to when he has had too much is when our patient complains."

"Mulci," Rentahs interrupted, "I have learned that they are called humans. But has anyone tried to get the names of our two guests?"

Mulci blushed a deep chocolate brown and said, "I apologize, Ren . . . Maili. The fighter of the two started that conversation himself, actually. His name is Anuk." The name came out sounding more like 'Ahneeyook.'

Mulci continued, "The unconscious one is named Hotchkins," which came out sounding more like 'Hawtch-kyins.'

Just then the chef arrived with dinner. The clear, resealable, and reusable bags full of food were placed on the table along with eating and drinking implements and condiments.

Some of the bags were steamy on the inside but with various cooked foods filling the majority of the bag. Some were clear and full of cooled fresh vegetables. Some had cold liquid, others hot. All were held to the table by tiny magnetic strips. After they had both taken time to make a minor assault on their dinner, Rentahs said, "Would you continue with your report please?"

"Of course," Mulci said around a mouthful and then continued exactly where she had left off. "The only way I can make sure Hotchkins is not receiving too much of the treatment is for him to tell me himself. And while he is unconscious, if he receives too much and gets nauseous like Anuk did, he will most likely attempt to discharge the contents of his stomach. In the case of Hotchkins though, that effort alone could kill him. Therefore, I dare not take that chance unless absolutely necessary. For now though, we will monitor and wait to see what happens."

"Excellent report," said Rentahs. "Did you have any problem creating atmosphere for them?"

"At first yes, but only because of difficulties getting access to an atmospheric processor."

"You must be making a joke. Please tell me you are or somebody in Environmental Control is going to help search the septic systems for Binqk bombs," Rentahs said only half jokingly.

"Don't hold it against them too much. We got one with plenty of time to spare. The processors did take heavy damage during the battle, remember." Rentahs did remember of course. Damage to his ship(s) and casualty reports he always remembered.

"Actually, the technician in E.C. just happened to be on my communications screen when the Master at Arms delivered that particular speech about how the alien had been treated," Mulci giggled.

"They were running just shy of enough to keep the ship caught up on clean air. After the next one was repaired, E.C. wanted to detoxify the entire ship's air supply before we would be allowed to create atmosphere, and he pointed out that the security boys did do one thing right. They found canisters of air for these humans and that the humans were already wearing their environmental suits. They could last for another shift if need be.

"Then they heard Master at Arms talk about searching the septic tanks in the background and suddenly they got really cooperative."

"I'm not surprised," laughed Rentahs. "So you have been able to provide quarters with a suitable atmosphere for them then?"

"Yes. And actually they breathe stuff very similar to ours. In fact we could share an atmosphere for short periods. Did I mention that? No? Except that instead of breathing in carbon dioxide and exhaling oxygen, they breathe in oxygen and exhale carbon dioxide."

"Mulci," Rentahs said disbelievingly, "are you twisting my upper elbow joint? I thought the only thing that could do that was plant life. At least that is what I learned in school."

"I learned the same thing," said Mulci. "But, the universe is a strange place. This is certainly going to raise ears in the scientific community."

"Make sure you have someone learning their language and teaching them ours," Rentahs said absentmindedly.

"I am learning their language as are two of my assistants, two of my students, and the Department Head of Communications and his staff.

"All of us will be helping teach the humans our language as soon we can," Mulci stated firmly. "The only exception is one of the two assistants to the Department Head of Communications. This is because his family, the Catchimikloflan, have not been noted historically as breeding for brains, but rather their ability to do menial work.

"However, the one most adept at their language and its nuances seems to be the yeoman assigned to the aliens. Her name is Tserofed. Her family name is

Yllekflan," stated Mulci. "She has a gift for both verbal and body languages." A brief pause and then, "She should be in either the psychology department, the communications department or both, with her natural abilities, but she seems to have been overlooked."

Rentahs caught the blatant hint without word or show, but did say, "Consider Tserofed to have been transferred if and as it pleases her. Make sure she understands that any training or material costs will come out of clan funds and she is not expected to recompense.

"Her training is to be considered highest priority by my personal order. I will make sure it is noted as such in my personal logs. This means that her instructors will make themselves available to her whenever she can schedule the time. Not the other way around. If her duties with the aliens require her to take extra time before any tests, her instructors are to allow it. No exceptions. Make sure her instructors fully understand this." Rentahs snickered at the situation in general. "If they have any questions send them physically and directly to me. They won't have any questions after that."

"Of that," Mulci said to herself, "I have absolutely no doubt."

Rentahs was ecstatically pleased. So pleased in fact that he said, "Mulci, I am releasing you from all other duties. I want you to make taking care of the humans your only responsibility."

"Warmth to your bed, Rentahs. I am greatly honored by this duty appointment."

"Excellent. And speaking of warmth, would you care to help me keep my bed warm for a shift?"

"Again, I am most honored, Maili."

"The honor is mine, Mulci."

Among Fombe it is rare not to share a bed. In fact, it is a form of torture for a Fombe to have to sleep alone. There is something deep in the Fombe psyche that tears at their minds when they are alone, especially when sleeping. Not to mention that they never, from the day they are born, sleep alone. The child sleeps with the parents and any older siblings. Visitors share the family bed, or there is always a large guests' bed that could hold an entire family.

Sleeping together, no matter what gender, is therefore the most natural thing in the universe to a Fombe. No less than two would ever sleep together if there were more than one. But it was not uncommon for groups of twelve or more to sleep together. Most strange to humans was that sex might or might not take place in any size group. Unlike humans, sleeping arrangements had very little or nothing to do with sex.

However, the offer the Admiral made had not in any way excluded sexual activity, and Mulci was well aware that any breeding between her family and Admiral Rentahs' would bring great tidings to both and most especially, their child, if any.

# CHAPTER 9

Eight shifts after the battle:

Mike Hotchkins drifted slowly back to consciousness. As he became aware of his body he regretted the previous nights debauchery and vowed never to drink so much again. This was absolutely and without a doubt the worst hangover he had ever had. He had not even opened his eyes yet, and the light filtering through his eyelids felt like twin ice picks stabbing through his eye sockets and into his brain.

Lying on his back, he moved to roll over in his bunk only to discover a grinding and agonizing shooting pain from his left arm just below the elbow all the way up to his shoulder joint. And the right side of his chest was a blaze of searing pain.

Slowly and carefully he raised his right arm up to place his hand on his aching head. Opening his eyes he found the right one would not open. He groaned in pain.

A familiar voice responded to his groan with. "Welcome back, Hotch."

"Anuk," Hotchkins managed to say. His mouth felt dry, his throat raspy, and his lips were chapped. Looking around at the unfamiliar room he inquired, "Where the hell are we?"

"We are in our cabin, aboard the Fombe ship Ttiflan, somewhere in null space, and headed for the Fombe capital world, wherever that is." Anuk went to the wall opposite Hotchkins bunk, did something, and returned with a tube of water and a straw for his friend. "Here Hotch, try to drink some of this—take it slow though—you have had quite a time."

Hotchkins took a sip and realized he was terribly thirsty. Taking a gulp he discovered a problem with swallowing—got some down the wrong tube—and went into a coughing fit so painful he passed out.

When he regained consciousness again, he found he was alone. Slowly and carefully he took stock of his battered body and tried to remember what had happened. His left arm had been broken when Anuk fell on him aboard the Hawking. The aliens had captured him and taken him to a shuttle of some sort. He remembered the debarkation maneuvers and acceleration. Then there had been multiple explosions and he was thrown to the deck where he banged his head. While that had been painful, it had not seemed to be a bad enough impact to have given him a concussion. Then there was heavy acceleration and he slammed his right side into the bunk. "That explains the ribs," he thought.

About that time he noticed he could barely breathe through his nose. Gasping through his mouth, he decided he could breathe through his nose a little, just not enough to keep him fully supplied with sufficient air. His nose was dramatically swollen but not tender. His right eye was completely swollen shut though it did not seem to hurt either.

Slowly and carefully he turned his head and looked around the cabin. The walls, floor, and ceiling were all a pearl white color and had no seams. There didn't appear to be any rivets or fastenings of any kind that he could see. It seemed to be made of one solid piece of material. The wall opposite him, where Anuk had gotten the tube of water, was the only spot he thought he could detect any kind of break in the material. There was an indentation about one half a meter tall by one half a meter wide, and looked maybe five or ten centimeters deep. There were two bunks in the room. A small table with a bench on either side was situated between the bunks. Each bunk had storage beneath it. Everything seemed to be made of the same material as the walls.

He took all of this in while trying to figure out just what he should be doing. On top of his list was getting something to drink. First priority of survival in any situation: Water, food, and shelter.

Finding the latches to the safety webbing holding him in the bunk was simple (at least he wasn't tied or locked down). He fumbled with the latches for a few seconds, then slowly, with great care and considerable pain, he pushed himself up to a sitting position. Dizzy from pain and exertion, he rested for a moment. While he rested and before making the attempt to cross the room, he tried to remember everything Anuk had told him about their situation.

Aboard the (Fom-Bay, was that right?) ship (Titty-flan?). Headed to their home world.

Another memory of something Anuk had said earlier surfaced in his mind, "We don't know if we are prisoners of war or dinner for these people."

That was an idea he could easily have lived without, he decided.

Suddenly the door to the "cabin" opened and Anuk casually thrust himself in. He was wearing some kind of apparatus just beneath his nose that appeared to be some form of re-breather supplying air directly to his nostrils. It was fastened around the back of his head.

Pulling the re-breather off, Anuk came to Hotchkins with a worried look on his face.

"Hotch," he said, "you shouldn't be sitting up just yet." The concern in his voice was genuine. "Please, let me help you lay back down before you cause yourself more injury."

"Water first," Hotchkins rasped past his dry throat and mouth.

"Of course, my friend," Anuk replied. Once again he went to the indentation at the far wall and returned with a tube of water and a straw. "Sip it slowly. You scared me silly last time, my friend."

"Sure, sure. Just let me have the damn water okay?"

While Hotchkins sipped his water, Anuk stored the re-breather in one of the storage cabinets under the far bunk. Then he went to the indentation again and returned with two tubes filled with something a disgusting greenish-brown color and sat down next to Hotchkins on the bunk.

"You must be famished," Anuk said, offering one of the tubes. "It looks nasty but actually tastes very good."

"What is it?"

"The Fombe call it 'mifp.' It is apparently their version of shipboard emergency rations. When you get to feeling better we can go to the galley for some real food."

"Whoa, slow down." Hotchkins was having problems deciding which of the two or three dozen questions to ask first. "Fum Bay?"

"It is pronounced 'Fom-bay.' But eat first Hotch and I will try to answer some of your questions while you eat."

Anuk opened the tube and handed it to Hotchkins who hesitantly tried a tiny nibble. "You're right, it's not bad."

"I told you," Anuk snickered. "Okay, where to start. First, you have been unconscious for nearly three days."

"Three days!" exclaimed Hotchkins. "What exactly happened?"

"You want the full version or the short, abbreviated, seven-hour account of the last three days?"

"Just the synopsis please."

" Okay. Do you remember the shuttle accident?"

"Yes, I think so. I definitely remember something about being on the shuttle and explosions and heavy acceleration and then another explosion. But that's about it."

"Well," continued Anuk, "the shuttle took three shots from our fighters before she made the mothership, Ttiflan. Just as we entered the hanger bay we took another shot and slammed into the deck. I think we had come in at much too high of a speed, though I have not been able to find out for sure yet. Language problems still. Then we bounced off another shuttle that was sitting on the deck and slammed into the bulkhead at the far end of the landing bay. We were lucky to have survived at all. The pilot and eight of the team they sent to the Hawking were killed instantly. Seventeen more of the Fombe are still in their infirmary."

"Anuk," Hotchkins said slowly, "far be it from me to complain about still being alive, but you seem to have walked away from the whole thing without a scratch."

Anuk looked decidedly uncomfortable but said, "I was knocked unconscious for a few hours. And had a couple of fractured bones in my right arm and hand."

"That was it? How did you luck out? But hold it, you're not even wearing a sling. And I have seen you use that hand. It didn't cause you any pain to use it or that arm. What the hell is going on?"

"Well, I um," Anuk stammered . . . "First Hotch, I owe you a thanks."

"For what?"

"For breaking my fall during the crash. You see, I landed on you and that saved me from any serious injury."

Several seconds passed without a word from either man. Finally Mike Hotchkins broke into laughter, grabbed his ribs in pain, and fell back onto the bunk giggling and complaining.

"Oh God that hurts. I gotta quit hanging around you, Anuk. First you fall on my arm and break it aboard the Hawking and now this. You keep falling on me and people will begin to talk. Ow, ow, ouch! Oh God it hurts to laugh," Hotchkins said as he continued to laugh.

Snickering, Anuk replied, "I will try to make this the last time." Then, "Hotch, are you ready to be serious now?"

"Yeah I guess we're in some serious trouble aren't we?"

"Less so than you might think. These people are not all bad. I have been learning some of their language and can get some questions answered. But I am talking 'baby talk' so to speak.

"They healed my broken arm and hand. Oh, their first attempt made me sick and throw up, but I could tell my arm was much better. So, when their doctor wanted to try again, I agreed. I think she turned down the power setting on whatever they used. But anyway she gave me five more treatments to the arm and a total of seven to my hand and I am healed!"

"Wait a minute," interrupted Hotchkins, "she? I have seen something of these beings and if I remember correctly, they wear clothes. Does 'she' have her 'genitalia' openly displayed for you? Or are you basing this gender decision on something else?"

"Well, um," Anuk blushed so much that even his mahogany skin pigmentation could not hide it. "She was very interested in comparative biology. Fombe morals are not quite like that of modern mainstream Earthers. They are not the least bit shy about seeing another's body or another seeing theirs."

"Do you mean, oww, ow, to say," Hotchkins managed to both laugh and say, "Ouch, that you have been playing doctor, oh . . ., oh . . ., ow, with their doctor? Oww! Oh God, that hurts! Oww! Oh, ouch."

"Yeah well, don't be asking me for pain pills," Anuk brooded.

"No seriously, Anuk. We need to learn all we can about these beings." A glint appeared in Hotchkin's eye as he asked, "So, was she sexy? Ow. God."

"You know," commented Anuk, "I can hardly wait for you to get well. Because the day the doctor says you're fit, I am going to beat you to a pulp."

41

"In the mean time," Anuk went on, studiously ignoring both Hotchkin's display of hilarity and his own desire to punch Hotchkins in the broken ribs. "While you just woke up, I have been awake for nearly thirty hours, and was working nearly twenty hours without any sleep before that little two hour nap. I have got to get some sleep! Can we go over what I have learned in a few hours, please?"

"Oh, sure!" retorted Hotchkins, "And just what in the hell am I supposed to do while you sleep? Count the imaginary rivets in the wall? While you have been traipsing about chasing alien women Anuk, I have been stuck in this cabin, which is pretty bland to look at mind you. It took all of two, maybe two and a half minutes to see it all and get bored."

"Oh bullshit Hotch. I was here within two minutes both of the times you regained consciousness. Or had that minor detail evaded you? Now relax, something will turn up for you to do."

"All right. You win. But you wouldn't happened to have smuggled a book along in your space suit wouldja?"

"No, but I did have a couple of dancing girls in there. If I can find where they went when we got here, I will send them your way, though I suspect they disappeared under the category of 'Captain's Spoils'."

Anuk yawned largely. "Not to worry though, you won't be bored long. Tserofed ought to be here any second to take you to the infirmary to heal those broken ribs and your broken arm."

Hotchkins found himself with too many questions to know where to start. He was saved from having to make the choice as the door to the cabin opened and in came one of the Fombe.

"Aw for crying out loud, haven't you people ever learned to knock?" Hotchkins complained not expecting any response.

"Hotchkins," Its accent and the re-breather in its nose hole making his name sound like 'Hawtchkyins.' "My here now, time known, required. You wake up. Must go heal."

Caught unawares, Hotchkins' mouth fell open.

"Hotch," said Anuk from his bunk, "meet Tserofed. Her job, from what I can tell, is to be our personal yeoman. So pick your jaw up off the deck and say hello."

"She spoke. She spoke in English!"

"Very good Hotch. She has had three days to learn some English while you slept. Now say 'hello' and go with her to the infirmary so I can get some sleep."

"Just promise me one thing Anuk," Hotchkins said only half jokingly, "that I am going to the infirmary and not the butcher shop. I just don't feel up to being the soup de jour."

"Hawtchkyins neehd heulp?" She asked, her accent making the human words difficult to understand.

Hotchkins did indeed need help. His broken left arm was totally useless for the zero G maneuvers required to navigate a ship in null space, where there was no acceleration and therefore no "gravity." His right arm wasn't much better off. Every time he tried to raise it to catch a grip it would send waves of rending pain up his side. Help was the last thing he wanted right now, but practicality persevered over pride.

"It looks like I don't have a choice," he grumbled.

"Okay, Hawtch." Tserofed said enthusiastically. Going to a drawer under his bunk she pulled a re-breather out and helped him to put it on.

Then she moved behind him, wrapped one long arm protectively around his shoulders and holding him firmly against herself, carried him off to the infirmary.

Shocked as he was at being hugged so intimately by a female, an alien female he reminded himself, he still took time to view his surroundings.

The door to their cabin was actually an air lock. No surprise there. Anuk took his re-breather off when he entered. Tserofed kept hers on when she came in then took it off outside the airlock.

Tserofed was removing her re-breather just outside the airlock as two more Fombe passed by in deep conversation.

Hotchkins was genuinely impressed with the grace that the Fombe exhibited when maneuvering a corridor. These people were definitely not "dirty feet" gone to space. They were born spacers.

The corridor outside was lined on three sides with handholds. The fourth side with a heavy black foam pad.

The foam side Hotchkins designated as "down," reasoning that if the ship were under acceleration that would be towards the rear of the ship or "down." Having a floor to walk on meant that they would be moving perpendicular to the line of acceleration. Following that reasoning, he determined they were most likely headed in toward the center of the ship.

Sick bays are always in toward the center of a ship. This provides the most protection for the wounded. "Well, that is the human way of looking at it," he reminded himself.

The black foam stood out quite well as it was the only material he had seen used to construct the ship that was not pearl white, making it easy to keep track of "down."

Two major junctions later, they turned left. At the next junction they went right and maneuvered through a massive airlock into the infirmary.

Tserofed released him when he grabbed a toehold. She made her way over to a desk containing another Fombe. They carried on an animated conversation, during which he was sure he heard his name. Then, the two Fombe ushered him into a back room and proceeded to strip him bare naked.

Curses, threats, and struggling availed him not as he soon found himself wearing only his birthday suit and hung by a toehold next to a diagnostic bed of some kind.

The receptionist focused all three eyes on him and said, "Hawtchkyins, Mife Poo Meehchoo," and left.

"Lady, I've no idea what you just said. But I would drink to it if I could."

Tserofed floated over to a cupboard on the far side of the room and returned with a tube of water. "Drink," she said thrusting the tube at him.

Rather than argue, he sipped and took the opportunity to study his guide.

She was more than two meters tall, her movements surprisingly graceful, if strange, due to the extra joints in arms and legs.

Still, in spite of the strange way she moved, even in zero gravity, something about her movements distinctly registered in his brain as female.

Another Fombe floated into the room and something about the way it moved registered as female as well.

"What the hell!" Hotchkins said out loud. "I haven't been in space that long."

They both looked at him and he blushed. His hands covered his loins without any conscious effort on his part. Quickly, he pushed that thought aside. Buck naked and about to be examined by an alien doctor was not the time to get caught with an involuntary erection.

"Focus," he thought furiously. "What are their features? What do they look like? Concentrate."

Their middle eye was larger than the other two. They seemed to use the center eye for focused attention and close work.

The other two eyes tracked independently of the center, but tracked together. They were farther apart than human eyes, giving them better binocular vision than humans.

Their ears were like small fans and flexible. They seemed to move with emotions like a form of body language.

The Fombe who had just entered approached him. Pointing at Hotchkins' chest it said "Hawtchkyins." Taking her hand and placing it on her own chest she said, "Mulci," with a facial gesture that approximated a smile.

Hotchkins pointed at himself and said, "Hotchkins," then pointed at her and said, "Mulci."

Mulci seemed jubilated at the immediate understanding. Bubbling over with happiness like a little girl who has discovered butterflies, she opened a cabinet in the wall and removed a device of some kind. Floating over to Hotchkins she held the instrument out for his inspection.

"Kleezprag," she said, pointing at the device with the other (seven-fingered!) hand. Then added, "heeuw ahrum," and pointed at the break in his left arm.

Made of the same pearl white material as everything else, the device was held by a pistol grip. Flowing from the top of the grip it extended up, out, and down around in front of the knuckles to a base that held a gold-colored pyramid. The tip pointed away from the operator and toward the patient. There were both finger and thumb triggers, marked blue and green respectively. Two dials near the thumb had markings on them he could not decipher other than that one was marked with red and the other with yellow.

But the most impressive feature was that it had a mini-holo screen set in the back of the handle. It measured approximately fifteen centimeters by fifteen centimeters by one centimeter thick. Mulci pointed the tip of the pyramid at Hotchkins' arm and turned one of the dials. Fascinated, Hotchins watched as a three-dimensional image of the bone and tendons in his arm appeared just above the screen. Using one of the dials, Mulci focused in on the break in the bone, getting a good look at it from several angles.

Hotchkins was as fascinated with the accurate three-dimensional image provided by the device as he was repulsed by the images of the break in his arm.

Mulci put the Kleezprag on a hook attached to her belt and took hold of Hotchkins' wrist. "Kklrenz impop. Tpailiu mextaph, oolnt," she said focusing all three eyes on his arm. "T'hyime owt Hawtchkyins. Oh-kay?"

With incredible speed her left hand lashed out and grabbed his left elbow. Just as Hotchkins realized what she was about to do, she did it; one quick yank and twist from her right hand simultaneously with one jerk and hold with her left. There was a loud "pop" from his broken arm that he felt as well as heard.

"Ahhh!" Hotchkins screamed.

Mulci and Tserofed both jumped back at his outburst. Six eyes coming to focus on him, pupils dilating as their owners drifted away from him.

"Hawtchkyins hurrt?" one of them, Mulci, asked. Something in the way she said it sounded worried. Hotchkins flushed red with embarrassment as he realized that it had not hurt. But they had not given him anything for pain. He had every reason to believe that setting a broken arm in that manner would hurt like hell. Yet, while he had felt the "pop" in his arm it had not been painful. His ribs hurt like hell from his own instinctive reaction to grab and hold his left arm with his right hand when he realized that Mulci was going to set the bone.

"Hmm," he had an idea. "Mulci, ribs hurt," he said pointing at his chest.

"No, Hawtch. Heawul arum nohw," Mulci insisted.

"No, no," Hotchkins interrupted. Pointing at his ribs again he said, "Ribs hurt! Kleezprag, no hurt."

"Hawtch! No rihb nohw! Arum!"

"Aw for crying out loud. Out of all the millions of beings required for a society that had developed to this level, and all the ships they must have in all the solar systems in all the galaxy, why did I have to get the one Fombe without enough brains to pick the dingleberrries out of her food?" Hotchkins complained more to himself than the two Fombe.

Tserofed floated closer and said, "Hawtchkyins, Kleezprag hno hurt smhal t'hyime. Arum nohw. Oh kay Hawtch?"

"Well, I guess since you put it that way, okay."

Mulci pointed the Kleezprag at his arm again and activated the imaging system. Again the three-dimensional image of his bones and tendons appeared. Moving it around she took a thorough look at how the bone was set. Lifting her ear, she glanced up at Hotckins with her small eyes. "Gooud. Oh kay Hawtch. Heeuw arum."

She pressed another trigger button and a targeting screen appeared imposed on the image of his arm. Four purple lines met in a tiny purple circle at the center of the image. She adjusted one of the dials and the image "sliced away" some of the bone tissue allowing an interior view of the damage at the target site.

Then Mulci pressed the thumb trigger and a golden beam of light was emitted from the tip of the pyramid and disappeared into the flesh of his arm. But in the image on her viewer, the golden light went clear to the target sight on the bone in his arm. And it itched! Lord how it itched. He tried to ignore it to think of something else. "What are they wearing? Concentrate!"

It was no use. Just as he reached the point that he couldn't stand it anymore and would make them stop, a wave of nausea swept over him. It washed over and through him, forcing him to go with the current, right on down to near unconsciousness. Darkness did not quite overtake Hotchkins.

"I sure hope you have a space sick bag around here." Even as he mumbled it he realized that the nausea was fading away. If he was lucky, he might not need one.

# CHAPTER 10

Several hours and eighteen treatments later Hotchkins felt like a new man. All that remained were some minor swelling and stiffness where the breaks had occurred. Mulci had explained that this would go away within a short time. But he was fine, aside from being exhausted and ravenously hungry.

Tserofed offered him a pouch of something vaguely orange in color. "Eeht. Chinch," and made eating gestures.

Hotchkins opened the end and sniffed warily. "It smells something like a cross between grapes and blackberries," he commented. Trying a tiny bit he found it tasted much like it smelled. "Good," he said rubbing his stomach and taking a large bite of the chinch.

By the time he finished the chinch he was getting sleepy. "I would like to go to my cabin now," he said around a yawn.

Tserofed looked at him and said, "Hawtchkyins, neehduh wharm. We keep wharm. Oh kay?"

Yawning again, Hotchkins said, "Yes, the temperature is quite comfortable. Warm, yes."

The last thing Mike Hotchkins remembered before he fell asleep was the two Fombe looking at him with their smaller pairs of eyes and at each other with their large center eyes.

Mike Hotchkins slowly and leisurely drifted from a deep relaxing sleep into wakefulness. He became aware that he was not alone. Unable to place her name but not feeling hurried to remember, he reached out his arm and upon feeling her body responding to his touch, he felt a familiar arousing sensation. A stray whiff of something briefly brushed his nostrils. His mind registered coffee and nutmeg. Cappuccino! His hand played a little lower on her abdomen. Again she responded. Again he felt his body's response to her. He pulled her closer to him and said, "Good morning," and opened his eyes.

Three green eyes set in a ruddy brown face surrounded by purple cilia where hair should have been stared back at him.

"Ahhhh!" Hotchkins screamed at the top of his lungs.

Flailing and flapping like an injured bird, he screamed and struggled to get out of the sleeping bag that held him. The Fombe in front of him screamed when he screamed. Then another scream and severe thrashing came from behind him, spooking Hotchkins into hysterical shrieking and writhing about.

All at once three individuals were floating around the room flapping their arms and demanding to know what was going on in their own respective languages. Not one of them was wearing a single stitch of clothing.

Several minutes later a much calmer group consisting of two Fombe females (there was no longer any doubt about that!) and one human male began discussing the situation.

Tserofed and Mulci were "waruming Hawtch's behd." They had explained this in such a way that he received the definite impression they felt it was some kind of an honor for them.

"Well," he thought, "when in Rome. Besides, we are all adults presumably and these are aliens after all. It's not like anything could happen." Looking into Tserofed's three eyes he was convinced.

They all crawled back into the sleeping bag again. Then a hand brushed him in an intimate manner and was gone. Hoping beyond hope that it was an accident, he ignored the matter.

"When do we go to the galley?" He asked.

Both of the aliens stared uncomprehendingly at him.

"The galley? Eat?" He said making eating gestures.

The hand came back. Only now instead of brushing lightly and going away, it was stroking him gently.

"Whoa, no you don't," Hotchkins stated loudly and firmly as he scampered out of the sleeping bag. "Ain't no way, no how! For all I know you could be the nubile virgin daughter of the Emperor of the Galactic Empire and it would be death by slow torture for me and annihilation for my planet just for me to touch you."

Searching through cupboards for clothing of some type—any type—he kept repeating for himself as much as the other two, "Just ain't gonna happen. No way. Not now, not ever. Nope. Just ain't gonna happen. No way. Where the hell are my damn clothes?"

Mulci came up to him and placed a hand on his shoulder. He slapped the hand away.

"Where . . . is . . . my . . . clothing . . . ?" Hotchkins said each word slowly and menacingly.

Mulci made her way over to a cupboard, opened it and withdrew a set of clothing for Hotchkins. Returning she handed them to him. While he dressed, she moved over to a panel, opened it, and made an adjustment to one of the controls inside. The panel then made an adjustment to the medications Hotchkins was receiving through the medical patch over his broken arm. Mulci closed the panel and went to the sleeping bag to check on Tserofed who seemed to be crying.

Hotchkins never got half his clothes on before the sedative Mulci dispensed to him took affect and he fell asleep again.

Hotchkins was waking up in a slow leisurely manner from deep slumber. He felt wonderfully lazy. Slowly he realized there was someone with him in bed. Even as the smile lit the corners of his face, his sleepy mind recognized the smell of coffee and nutmeg. This was just like that crazy dream . . .

Hotchkins eyes snapped open to see a monster with coffee brown skin, three eyes, and purple cilia.

"Son of a bitch!" he yelled. Tserofed's eyes snapped open as she started awake. "This is getting real old, real fast," Hotchkins continued. "Now listen. I realize that someone has beaten you with the ugly stick really bad, but going outside your own species is not going to help. Especially not with me. What you need to do is find yourself a nice blind Fombe male."

Finding the correct cupboard with his clothing, he pulled them out and said, "Can I go back to my cabin now?"

After he dressed, Mulci guided him back to his own cabin in silence. She didn't even look at him. Hotchkins didn't mind. He was too busy trying to figure out what he would tell Anuk if he asked where Hotchkins had been.

His face felt hot at just the thought. The whole thing was terribly embarrassing. He found he was sweating and had a mild case of the shakes. The last thing in the galaxy he wanted was for Anuk to find out. He would never hear the end of it.

Mulci stayed outside as he cycled through the lock to his cabin.

Entering he saw Anuk seated at the table looking at a three-dimensional schematic. Hotchkins normally would have been fascinated by the schematic, but recent events kept his mind occupied. He quickly looked away.

Anuk looked up and said, "Hotch! How are you feeling?"

"Er, fine. Just fine," Hotchkins said heading toward his bunk.

"It's almost time to eat," Anuk said. "You hungry? Want to go grab some chow?"

"No thanks," Hotchkins said blushing and trying really hard not to look at Anuk. "I just need some sleep," Hotchkins said lashing himself into his bunk.

"Where have you been?" Anuk asked.

"The infirmary, remember? They patched me up."

"All this time? Hotch, it's been almost two days."

Hotchkins could not quite put his finger on what made him think so, but he had the distinct impression that Anuk was struggling not to laugh. Guilt he decided. Useless guilt. Forget about it. "Well, I don't know how long it took to do the actual healing work, but they knocked me out for a while afterward. I was asleep."

Just then a soft chime sounded.

Anuk ignored the chime and said, "Asleep? All this time?"

"What do you want me to say? Yes! I was asleep the whole time," Hotckins said hotly.

"That must be why you are so tired," Anuk remarked. "Are you sure you don't want to go get a bite to eat?"

"No, thank you. I'm really not hungry, just tired. You go ahead."

"Suit yourself," Anuk said stepping into the airlock.

As Hotchkins manuevered himself just above his bunk, he listened to the sound of the inner door closing then the airlock cycling. The outer door opened then shut.

And while he was not certain, he thought, for just a second, that he heard the sound of laughter out in the corridor.

Seventeen shifts later, Hotchkins and Anuk were enjoying a meal together and debating which was best for breakfast—plitzbah with gutu sauce or a Denver omelette. Hotchkins was pointing out that the plitzbah had more of the "meat-like stuff," and that with the gutu sauce it tasted nearly the same as a Denver omelette, perhaps better.

Tserofed sat next to Anuk and raising one ear said, "Another fight?"

"No fight," Anuk said, "just one mans opinion that garbage tastes like food and vice versa."

Now Tserofed's ears were both up. She just sat there waiting for an explanation, looking at Anuk with the center eye and Hotchkins with the other two. Hotchkins glared at Anuk and Anuk tried not to laugh. When no explanation was forthcoming Tserofed finally said, "Two shift rotations we home. Good food then," she said staring at her food like it might explode at any second.

The Fombe had made clear with star charts where their home system was. They could not seem to understand the reluctance and then refusal on the part of Hotchkins and Anuk to tell them where the human home system was.

"Tserofed, why have the Fombe captured us?" asked Hotchkins.

"Cap-tured? What mean?"

"Why did you take us from Hawking ship to Ttiflan ship?" tried Anuk.

"Hawking ship no atmosphere soon. We not take, Hotch, Anuk . . ." Tserofed searched for the words but did not know them yet. Instead, she placed her hands around her own throat, rolled up all three eyes, and collapsed onto the table.

"I see," said Anuk as he hid a smile and a chuckle behind his hand.

"Yes, but," asked Hotchkins, "why are we still with the Fombe? Why have you not let us rejoin our people?"

"You go people anytime," responded Tserofed. "I show you air lock."

"Oh very funny, Tserofed. Very funny," Hotchkins grumbled.

Both Tserofed and Anuk were trying really hard not to break up laughing.

"But if we want to go back to our people you will let us?" asked Hotchkins.

"Hotch, Anuk got ship?"

"Of course not. What kind of dumb question is that?"

"You not tell where home. We cannot take home. You no ship? You walk or no go."

"She's got you there Hotch," Anuk laughed.

# CHAPTER 11

T hree weeks after the battle, the Bismarck and the Nimitz (with the captured alien ship in tow), arrived at the shipyards in orbit around planet Earth's only moon, Luna.

Even before they made orbit, Admiral Price received a message that his presence, as well as that of Commander Andreiovich, was requested and required for a meeting with the president of the Democratic Earth Societies.

The Admiral's personal shuttle landed without incident. The occupants were escorted to the entrance of the Cheyenne Mountain military complex. Once inside, they were finger printed, underwent retinal scans, and tested with DNA to assure they were who they claimed to be.

From there, they were escorted past the massive vanadium steel doors where they underwent another identity check, before an elevator descent that took them deep beneath the heart of the mountain.

Eventually they found themselves ushered into a lavish office to meet with Lao Chin, President of the Democratic Earth Societies.

Looking up from his desk the President said simply, "Gentlemen, welcome. Please, have a seat. May I offer you something? I have a fully stocked bar and I can have my chef prepare nearly anything you would like to eat. I know that shipboard food can sometimes be lacking in quality."

Admiral Christopher Price felt the need to get on with this debriefing quickly, but obviously the president did not. "Earl Grey Tea will suffice, Mr. President and thank you, Sir."

"Certainly Admiral, but may I call you Chris?"

"Of course, Mr. President."

"That's better. How about you, Alexi? May I call you Alexi?"

"Certainly, coffee with cream please, Mr. President."

After serving them both, the president sank into his chair and nursed his ginger ale with a twist of lemon before proceeding.

"Gentlemen, I have of course, read your reports and those of your department heads. You seem to have had quite an encounter out there. But I would like to hear in your own words what happened. That, and clarify some of the details. Not being a military man myself, there are a few things I am on unsure footing about how to interpret. For instance, your reports both indicate that the aliens fired upon the Stephen Hawking twice before any action was taken against them."

"Mr. President," Admiral Price considered his words carefully. "The first laser shot at the Hawking was an x-ray laser at such a low power, even Abe Matthews, the Hawking's first officer, did not believe it was meant to cause any harm or damage."

"I understand that Chris, but why would they fire such a low power beam—not once but twice no less—and then, as the saying goes, 'shoot to kill'?"

"I cannot answer that. But detailed analysis of the records of the event showed that the second shot was at the same low power, non-lethal setting. Then, for no apparent reason, the power output of the laser shot off the scale. Examination of the long-range sensor data afterward indicates that they burned out their equipment with that shot. And my science officer suggested, after examination of the records, that the laser was broadcasting prime numbers at the Hawking's bridge. Anyway, at that point, we scanned the Hawking and determined that she was dead in space. I then determined this was indeed an attack."

"I see," said the president, "and when your cyberfighters attacked the alien shuttle . . . ?"

"I sent the cyberfighters to defend the Hawking and any of her crew left alive after the alien attack," Price said defensively.

"Did you, at that point, have any reason to believe any of the Hawking's crew were still alive?"

"Mr. President, if you are going to make, or are hinting at some kind of accusation, please just make your accusation, Sir."

"I am sorry, Chris. I did not mean to sound like I was making any accusations. As a politician and not a military man the way I phrase things can be well, misunderstood shall we say, by a military mind."

"Apology accepted Mr. President," said Price formally. "But know this, Sir, as a military man and not a politician, I say what I mean and mean what I say."

"Here now Chris, let's not butt heads. Again, I am not here to debate with you or accuse you. I merely want to clarify the facts."

"Then, Sir, I will answer you directly. I had no reason to believe that all of the personnel from the Hawking were dead. Further, in my judgment, I believed it would definitely not be in the greater interests of the DES for any of the equipment or personnel from the Hawking to be captured by the aliens. Therefore, I took steps to avoid that result."

"Very good. Thank you, Chris." The president shifted his attention to Commander Andreiovich.

"Alexi," he continued, "while I do not hold you responsible for the damage to the Bismarck, I would like to hear your opinion as to why Captain Hiemler would take on two-to-one odds with an unknown such as the alien ships."

"Mr. President," Alexi said with considerable formality, "with all due respect Sir, I cannot and will not speak disparagingly of my former commander."

"Then may I suggest you speak from your training, your personal knowledge of the events, and your heart, Alexi. I have no desire to disparage your Captain Hiemler either."

"Sir," Alexi continued formally, "Captain Hiemler stated that he believed the alien ships to be roughly equivalent to our standard heavy cruisers. To the best of my knowledge he determined this by what our science officer could tell from scans of the alien's weaponry. Since the Bismarck is one of the heaviest battleships ever built by any of the human colonies or Earth herself, it should have been more than able to take on two heavy cruisers, Sir."

"At ease, Commander. This is an informal debriefing, remember?"

"Mr. President," interrupted Admiral Price, "you keep reminding us that this is an informal debriefing, yet you insist upon making both the Commander and myself defend our positions. And in the Commander's case, you ask him to defend the position of his deceased commanding officer. I request to know to what end, Sir? I insist that you either come to the point and make your accusations or let this 'informal' debriefing go public. Commander Andreiovich was under my command, as was Captain Hiemler. If you intend to accuse any of the officers under my command of any form of impropriety, misuse of authority, negligence, or any other action deemed immoral or illegal, I insist that you tell me now or declare what charges you intend to press."

"Very well Admiral," the president said seriously. "While I do not hold with it, there has been some discussion in the senate that this battle with the aliens was a military ploy to increase the failing military budget."

"Mr. President," Admiral Price said with barely controlled rage, "these aliens attacked and killed the entire crew of the Stephen Hawking without any provocation, nearly two hundred men and women. They then boarded the Hawking and stole her navigational computers. When my cyberfighters were en-route to the Hawking, they were fired upon with atomic weapons. That is hardly a 'peaceful' action. And again, without any provocation."

"Please Admiral," the President said, "I understand your position, and personally I refuse to believe you would have anything to do with such a plot. But there are those in the senate who hold a different point of view." Taking a deep breath and letting it out slowly, the President continued. "Admiral, Commander, I need to get a feel for how you will respond to these accusations from the senate. The politics of this encounter are extremely volatile right now."

"Perhaps, Mr. President," Admiral Price interjected, "it would be best if you informed us of what these accusations are."

"Very well Admiral. In a nutshell: Some suggest the possibility that the Hawking took a shot at the aliens and because of distance and angle neither the Nimitz nor Bismarck could tell. Or, that one or both ships saw the shot and wiped it from the official records.

"Further, that the two unaccounted-for personnel from the Hawking were actually found but that they intended to tell the truth about the actions taken by their captain and yourselves, and were subsequently made to disappear.

"In addition, the two missiles armed with nuclear warheads were only electromagnetic pulse bombs that the aliens fired in front of and not at, the cyberfighters. They were *not* meant to destroy but to delay and/or disable without killing; therefore, your cyberfighters attacked without due provocation.

"Further, Captain Hiemler attacked two ships at once instead of merely keeping between them and the Nimitz for the sole purpose of starting a war with these aliens.

"And after the death of his captain, Commander Andreiovich went on to attack an already disabled alien ship with full knowledge that it was disabled.

"In essence gentlemen, they are accusing you of starting a war for your own purposes."

Commander Alexi Andreiovich leapt to his feet in a storm of fury. "Of all the asinine, pinheaded, shit for brains concepts I have ever heard, this takes the cake!"

"Commander!" barked the admiral. "At ease."

"But sir, how can they even suggest . . . ?"

"At ease Commander!" bellowed Price. "Now!"

"Aye, Sir." Alexi said as he took his seat.

"Mr. President," Admiral Price said behind carefully controlled anger, "how can they even suggest such a thing? We confirmed that our colony and space station were both destroyed. And the colony on the planet was destroyed in such a manner as to leave our high-tech equipment undamaged, but the people dead, so that they might return and take advantage of our technology."

"Admiral," the president said grimly, "your sensor scans of the alien ships and the sensor data sent from the space station just before it was destroyed show a discrepancy. It is not all together certain that these aliens you encountered were of the same race as the ones who destroyed our colony and space station. They do not show the same design parameters or I am told, the same energy signature."

Admiral Price felt as if he had just been kicked by a mule. He needed to sit down and take in that particular statement. Glancing over, he saw that Alexi had gone white and was staring blankly at nothing in particular.

"Mr. President," Admiral Price finally managed to say. "Setting aside the astronomical odds that we would encounter two intelligent alien races in such a short time span and in the same system—no matter who they are—we took no provocative action until fired upon."

"I believe you Chris, I truly do. But I wanted you to be aware of the political situation and what you will be up against," said the President earnestly. "This is why I cannot allow either of your crews to take shore leave just now. The press would be all over them. One wrong word, one small miss-statement, or one misguided brag from a sailor in a bar would be snatched up by the press and blown all out of proportion."

"I see your point Sir. Thank you for clarifying the situation."

"And now gentlemen would you care for refills? I do have a few more questions, but not nearly such sensitive ones. And I really would like to return to a more informal style for the remainder of this debriefing."

Alexi glanced at the nearly empty cup in his hand, decided he could use another, and gulped the rest before holding the cup out for the president to refill.

The president waited until both men had had an opportunity to take a drink from their cups before continuing. "Alexi, after the second exchange of fire with the two alien ships what happened exactly?"

"Well Mr. President, the second of the two ships moved off. We kept a watch on it until it created a jump point and left the system. The first ship was apparently dead in space.

"Realizing we had an invaluable opportunity for gaining information, I ordered boarding parties to the alien ship. Their orders were to attempt to offer aid and assistance, if possible, to any living aliens they found and determine whether we could salvage the alien ship and bring her back to Earth.

"Unfortunately, all thirty two of the living aliens they came across died shortly thereafter, most from their wounds. The remainder died from unknown causes. Our own medical personal had no idea how to treat them. While similar to ours, their biology is still radically different. We determined that the ship itself could be towed back with some effort and made repairs to both the Bismarck and the alien ship to prepare for the jump back to Earth."

"Excellent, Alexi. Chris, anything to add?"

"Well," Admiral Price started in, "after the alien we were chasing got away by making a jump we returned to a location near the Bismarck and retrieved our cyberfighters, making certain the Bismarck herself was in no danger. We sent repair crews over to the Bismarck and the alien ship to help prepare it for towing home.

"We also had those shuttles bring the Bismarck's wounded to sick bay on the Nimitz, their own sick bay having been almost completely destroyed in the battle.

"After conferring with Alexi about the condition of the Bismarck, we agreed that she was in no shape to tow another vessel through a jump point, but would be able to make the jump herself.

"Given the choice between towing the Hawking home or the alien home, we agreed that the alien ship was far more valuable as a resource. But, the Hawking should not be left for the aliens to return and recover. Therefore, I ordered the destruction of the Hawking."

"Chris," the President asked, "were you certain there was no way to repair the Hawking?"

"She was a dead hulk Sir. Her hull was intact but her electronics were all fried. Believe me, I would have liked to bring her home. But she would need a complete refit from a shipyard before she could fly again. The problem was not that she was dead, but that while all of her circuits were fried, they were still an accurate map of our technology. Anyone with the time and incentive could have studied her and figured out exactly how she worked."

"I see," said the president. "Well, we seem to have covered all of the major points I needed to discuss. You gentlemen could use some de-stressing. Why don't I mix up a large batch of margaritas and we all go jump into my private hot tub? I'll have my chef prepare us some lunch and bring it in. But one thing I want to make perfectly clear first. I do not allow business discussions in my hot tub. Understood?"

# CHAPTER 12

The Binqk Imperial City was not located on any world. Roughly eight hundred and fifty earth years ago the Binqk, being both warlike and paranoid, built their Imperial City in space. Experience had proven that the bottom of a gravity well is not a safe place to have a government. Lavish, spacious, and quite probably the most heavily defended and fortified location in the known galaxy, the city was the size of a small moon; continually growing and expanding as the bureaucracy expanded to meet the day-to-day business of running an interstellar empire.

In the center of all of this, in the safest possible location, were both the living area and Hall of Audiences for the Binqk emperor.

The Emperor stopped in front of a reflecting device to make certain its appearance was acceptable. Face and head both royal blue with just the right amount of slime, it thought to itself. Mouth green, teeth properly sharpened, metallic gold body, and enough slime on my foot so I leave a proper trail. Yes. I am ready to give an audience.

Emperor Pishmah Umselat Bourbaitoo III was not happy. "My advisers," it began, "this had better not be some trivial matter. I was in the middle of a game of Chetspau, and winning!"

"Indeed not my Liege," responded Yomin, both trusted advisor and Minister of Security. "It is of the utmost importance."

Pishmah settled down with a sigh of disgust. "Go ahead then."

"Liege, the Fombe fleet sent to Psht Phas Five, or what is left of it, has returned."

"What is left of it? Then our plan worked? Our agent successful?" Pishmah was intrigued.

"They encountered the humans. Our agent got one message out that said the Fombe and the humans refused to fire at each other. The agent was going to take action to encourage them to fire."

"Yomin old friend," Pishmah condescended, "you worry too much. Obviously, whatever our agent did was successful."

"Liege, the Fombe ship that had our agent on board has returned. According to the Fombe Ambassador to the Galactic Council, our agent was caught, tried, and convicted of sabotage and treason while aboard the Fombe vessel."

"Issue a 'denial of responsibility' for its actions. Inform them that we in no way condone any acts done by Special Representative Chok; that this is a Binqk matter and have our agent extradited immediately."

"Liege, I cannot."

"What? And why not?"

"Our agent did not return with them. They carried out the sentence aboard ship. The sentence was 'death'."

Pishmah turned violet with rage. "They murdered our Special Representative?"

"My Liege," Yomin interrupted, "according to the council, the Fombe were well within their legal rights."

"This is outrageous! Yomin is the council ready to make a stand regarding our response to this murder?"

"The council will not allow a war with the Fombe over this matter. We can still proceed with the war planned against the humans, though. However, it is doubtful now that we could get the Fombe on our side as planned. But if we are lucky, we may drag them into the war as our enemy and not have to cross them later."

Pishmah's slug-like body wriggled with pleasure before turning to his top military leader. "What a delightful notion. Mek, issue a statement to the Fombe and the council that we consider the murder of our Special Representative to be a terrible act of cowardice. Make a formal request for the council to levy sanctions against the Fombe for this murder. Inform them that the Binqk—being both a peaceful and merciful people—will take no aggressive action at this time.

"However, any further hostile or aggressive acts toward Binqk citizens by the Fombe will be considered grounds for war and will be treated as such."

"As you wish," responded Mek.

"Admiral Eenvupe," Pishmah said changing the subject, "how is the search for the human colonies coming?"

"My Liege, using the star chart from the human probe we managed to locate their home planet. Using that as a base point, we sent probes to nearly two hundred type G stars in that general vicinity of the galaxy."

"Yes, yes. What does it mean?" Pishmah asked impatiently.

"Three of our probes have discovered colonies. Two probes were destroyed from an unknown source. One probe was intercepted by a human ship and self-destructed. We have not received any telemetry from the remaining probes as of yet. Most have not reached their target systems, however."

"Our fleets?" Pishmah inquired.

"Our fleets stand ready to attack at your command, my Liege."

"Not just yet, Admiral. Soon though, very soon. I wish to find out more about how many colonies the humans have and where they are located. Then, as we exterminate the humans on the planet, we can release the information to the council after the fact, and claim they were destroying an atmosphere suitable for us. That should be enough for the council to decide to stay out of this, don't you think?"

"My Liege," Mek said carefully, "we might get the council to believe this story once more. Twice more would cause too much suspicion among the other delegates. The council might take an emergency vote to move against us."

"It only has to work once more," Pishmah wriggled. "Then, with the human's proven history of poisoning planets habitable by others, the council should be, if not actually on our side, then at least willing to stay out of our way."

As the brilliance of the plan dawned on the Imperial Advisors, they all wriggled with pleasure.

"Brilliant!"

"Excellent plan my Liege!"

"Sheer genius!"

"Truly remarkable!"

Pishmah took great pleasure in the plan he had devised, as well as in the accolades he was receiving because of that plan.

# CHAPTER 13

$A$board the Confederated Human Colonies carrier ship, Alabama, a message was received by the communications officer on duty. The communications officer, shaken by the message, referred to his duty shift supervisor for instructions. That worthy woke up his commanding officer and, after a serious chewing out, was relieved to get rid of this particular "hot potato."

From there, the message moved swiftly up through the hierarchy of the ship until it reached its intended recipient.

Allison Susan McCallister, President of the Confederated Human Colonies, had been quite surprised by the personal call from Lao Chin, President of the Democratic Earth Societies.

She accepted the call in her office and after the initial formalities asked simply, "Why have you called me directly, Sir? Have you forgotten that we have official channels for our respective governments to communicate?"

"Madam President," Lao Chin began. He paused and tried again. "I have information that could be of utmost importance to the entire human race. Because of the highly volatile nature of this information, I felt it best to speak directly to you."

"Well then Mr. President, perhaps you had best divulge that information."

"Madam, oh damn. Will you please call me Lao? And do you go by Allison?"

"I go by Madam President. Now please get to the point of your call."

"Very well then." Lao Chin's nervousness had nothing to do with her frigid response. "Madam President, a few months ago, one of our colonies and their orbital support station were destroyed by what appeared to be an alien race. We sent a small fleet of one science ship and two support ships to investigate. Our science ship encountered extraterrestrials. They were then attacked and their crew killed.

"The ship was left intact. Our scientists think they wanted to study our technology. The methods they used on the planet were the same kill the inhabitants leave the technology.

"Our two support ships engaged two of the alien ships in an attempt to keep our technology out of their hands. Our people barely prevailed.

" I feel this is a clear and present danger to the entire human race. Would you agree that the petty bickering of our two human societies should take a back seat long enough to hear me out?"

The sobering effect of his account was evident on her face. Allison McCallister sat down in her chair. Several seconds passed before she said, "Mr. unh, Lao." She was visibly shaken now that she realized he was serious. "You have evidence, of course?"

"We have ample evidence, Madam President," Lao Chin sighed. "We managed to capture one of their ships in the course of the battle. We also have multiple dead alien bodies from that ship."

"Dear God! It's true then," she said. "Okay Lao, you have my attention. And I go by Ally. But mind you, I do expect to have your evidence verified."

"Certainly, Ally. Bring all the scientists and equipment you need. Any new technology or information we find aboard will be shared with both of our peoples. But, I believe we should keep this as quiet as possible for now, on a need to know only basis. Don't you agree?"

"Absolutely! The public should be shielded from this for the time being. We don't need to start a panic. What do you recommend?"

"You discretely send a team of scientific and military investigators here. Working together with our people as a team, we study the aliens, their technology, and our data on the alien's tactics. We can work together to our mutual benefit."

"Lao, are you certain this wasn't all some misunderstanding? I mean, if they truly are alien, mistakes and misunderstandings are bound to happen."

"Ally," Chin said, "in the first contact with us they fired without warning and killed nearly forty five thousand people on the planet and in the orbital support station. Then, in the second contact, the one with our science and support ships, they attacked again without provocation or warning. Three of their warships attacked a lone science vessel and killed the entire crew of nearly two hundred. Both the colony on the planet and our science ship were destroyed in such a way as to leave the people dead, but the equipment intact."

"Okay, I guess there is no misunderstanding that," McCallister replied.

"Ally, we need to beef up both of our fleets. Let's be honest. Because of the war, ships are few and far between these days. Any ideas on how to build up our respective militaries without raising too many questions from the public?"

"Nope. But I do have a crazy idea how we might get away with it, nonetheless." She paused, reconsidered, and then forged ahead with her idea. "Six months of peace between our peoples have not yet healed all the wounds. It would be a dangerous game, but we could create political tension between our governments. Have a few minor 'incidents' of aggression each way. Each can claim that the peace is falling apart and point their finger at the other side. Create a 'fear of attack' then, use that as an excuse for military buildup."

"Ally, that is not a crazy idea. That is an absolutely insane idea! We dare not create another war between our peoples. It is the last thing we need right now. And what you propose is bringing us again right to the edge of war."

"Lao, I need to discuss this with my advisors. I will set up one terminal at this end for a permanent scramble to only receive from terminals using your personal code. I suggest you do the same at your end. Shall we speak again tomorrow at say, one o'clock PM GMT? That will give us both some time to come up with another plan."

"Agreed, I will call then. And thank you, Ally."

Ally signed off and became President McCallister again. President McCallister sat quietly staring at the blank screen for a few seconds. Then her eyes focused and she touched a button on her desk. Seconds later, her personal secretary's face appeared on the screen. "Yes, Madam President?"

"Bruce, I need the Vice President and the Secretary General. Then get my Security and Science advisors. Next, get me Admirals Hurley and Brave Eagle, and the Captain of the ship that shot the—whatever that thing was they are claiming was of alien origin. I need all of them either physically in my office or linked into a secure conference call in one hour. Understood?"

"Understood Madam President."

One and one half hours later, President McCallister had finished replaying her conversation with President Chin to her staff.

General confusion followed. Questions fired back and forth. She allowed it to go on for a few short minutes and then stood up. "People, people!" She leaned on the table and said in a loud commanding voice, "I want order right now."

At one hundred seventy centimeters tall and seventy-two kilos, McCallister was a 'sturdy' woman. Strenuous exercise being her favorite stress reducer, she worked out regularly. The bit of gray at the temples of her dark red hair, a testament of her term of service as president through two long wars.

"Admiral Brave Eagle, you look like a man with something to say."

"Thank you, Madam President. I cannot help but wonder if this might all be some elaborate ruse. They could capture our top military and scientific experts in a single blow and build up their navy while we sit back feeling safe, only to attack us at their leisure with a superior naval force."

"I think not, Admiral," interrupted Artemus O'Toole, the Presidential Science Advisor. "We have what is the remains of a probe of some sort that is not of human origin. Recently, it appeared out of Null space near the Eridani system. We detected the incursion by sheer accident, tracked the object that came through and when it entered the system, we intercepted it."

"And blew it up!" said Vice President Leo Walsh.

"Sir," Admiral Hurley began, "the object fired upon us with an x-ray laser, a weapon designed to kill the crew and leave the ship intact. We were lucky our force shields held as long as they did. That thing would have killed the entire crew within another fifteen seconds. Our return volley was set to hit the object with minimum power on the propulsion unit only. It should not have blown up. It had to have self destructed."

"My point," interrupted O'Toole, "is this: We found a probe of alien origin. The DES is claiming to have been attacked by aliens. I do not think this is a coincidence. It could well be that an alien race is expanding in our direction of the galaxy."

"Bullshit," Admiral Brave Eagle said simply.

"People," interjected the President, "I happen to believe President Chin's story. I do not trust the DES any more than you do. However, I dare say that Chin believes what he told me. And I think, if he is not being misled by his people, that he is correct. This is a clear and present danger to the entire human race. Not just the DES or the CHC but the entire human race. Now, I want some answers. Just what in the hell are we going to do about it?"

# CHAPTER 14

Forty-one shifts after the battle:

"Tserofed!" Mike Hotchkins hurried to catch up with her. "What's going to happen to us today?"

"What you mean, Hotch?" she asked.

"When we get to your capital city I mean. What is going to happen to Anuk and myself?"

"Nothing happen you and Anuk," Tserofed told him. "You and Anuk go Leader of Clans, Chief, King, Captain? of Fombe. Talk. Nothing happen."

"But we have been on this ship for days. The captain could have spoken to us anytime. Why wait until we reach the capital city?"

Tserofed snickered and said, "Not Captain of Ttiflan ship, captain of all Fombe."

Anuk was relaxing in his sleeping bag. He had been down in engineering several times attempting to learn about Fombe engineering style and techniques. As eager to learn as to help, Anuk had shown them a hand-drawn schematic of a still and with Tserofed acting as translator, had gotten across the concept of 'the mash.'

The Fombe engineers had been delighted with his descriptions. The shift leader had excitedly grabbed Anuk by the arm, and to the obvious enjoyment of all the Fombe engineers, brought him to a locker, which they opened to show off their zero gravity still.

"I will be dipped in shit," Anuk said in astonishment. Then laughing, "I guess engineers are the same in any society." With that, he reached up and slapped the shift leader on the back.

A well-meaning gesture that took Tserofed's help to get across that it was a friendly action and not an insult to the still or its owners.

The Fombe were eager to share both his ideas on improvements for the still and the bounty provided by it. So, when Hotchkins excitedly burst into their quarters, Anuk was nearly finished with the liter of alcohol the engineers had insisted on sending with him, and he was feeling pretty good about life in general.

"Whoa Hotch," Anuk slurred, "and you complain about the Fombe never knocking! Ah, well. Have a drink Hotch, ole' buddy." Anuk tossed the bag of alcohol to his friend.

Hotchkins caught the bag but did not drink. "Christ on a rocket. You sure picked a lousy time to get drunk."

"No time like the present, buddy. Now c'mon, drink up or pass it back."

"Anuk, do you know what is going to happen when we reach the capital city today?"

"Oh, let me guess. You found out that we are going into the stew pot after all?" Anuk started giggling at his own joke.

"This is serious Anuk! We are going to meet the Fombe leader."

"So? What'sa big deal?" Anuk laughed. "We meet some dignitary from the city, tell him our people mean no harm to his, he says we are alright in spite of being short one eye, two each knees, elbows, fingers, and toes."

"Damn it, Anuk! Will you listen to me? We are not meeting some minor functionary. We are to meet with the Fombe Emperor.

"Their Emperor?" Anuk asked dazedly.

"I'm not sure if Emperor is correct. I don't know if we have the correct title in our language. But whatever the proper title, this guy is in charge of all of the Fombe."

"All of them?" Anuk had stunned realization written all over his face.

"Yes!" Hotchkins reiterated. "Anuk, emperors have a tendency to leave people dead for being minor irritations. I couldn't even get along with Roberts back on the Hawking without getting in trouble. And with you drunk, oh dammit. We are so screwed."

"You are right about one thing," Anuk said seriously. "I picked a lousy time to get drunk. And unless the Fombe have something like coffee, you will be right about one other thing too. We are screwed."

"Friend Anuk go engineering this shift," Mulci observed smiling. She also assured them she had just what Anuk needed. With the touch of a few buttons on the display screen, the cabinet dispensed a tube full of something pink. Hotchkins thought it looked like a pink peppermint-flavored antacid his grandparents had always kept in their medicine cabinet.

Mulci held it out towards Anuk and made a scissors motion at the two—thirds level. "Drink here. Stop."

Anuk took the tube, thought for a second, and looked at Tserofed. "Does she want me to drink one-third and leave two-thirds?"

Hotchkins jumped in. "No, drink two-thirds and leave one-third."

As Tserofed got into a discussion with Mulci in their native tongue, Anuk and Hotchkins got into a debate in English. Eventually, Anuk settled the argument by opening the packet and drinking one-third.

Mulci and Tserofed both saw it happen with their two smaller eyes while finishing their own discussion. Mulci said something the humans could not understand that caused Tserofed to laugh. Then, "Anuk, taste bad?"

Suddenly Anuk's pupils dilated. His eyes grew wide and his face screwed up and turned red. It seemed every muscle in his body had tensed up. "Yawwgawd! Blech! Oh, that is nasty!" Grabbing his stomach, he continued making spitting noises and complaining.

He still had not gotten past the taste, but something he was aware of on the periphery of his mind was trying to get his attention. Mulci, Tserofed, and Hotchkins holding their stomachs in pain and laughing.

"It's not funny," Anuk stated indignantly.

The other three laughed for a few more seconds then it started to wind down. The laughing had almost died out when Hotchkins did a fair imitation of Anuk's reaction to the pink substance—including sound effects.

Again the trio all laughed themselves into convulsions. Anuk watched calmly for a moment, then giggled. Within a few seconds all four of them were laughing themselves silly.

As the laughing wound down, Anuk handed Mulci the tube. "No," Mulci said refusing to take it. Then she smiled and did her own imitation of Anuk's reaction complete with sound effects.

The laughing was not nearly as long or as heartfelt this time in spite of the quality of her performance.

Again, Anuk tried to hand back the tube. Again, she refused it. Laughing she said, "Anuk drink," and made the scissors gesture at the halfway mark.

"Oh, no! I am not drinking that stuff again."

Mulci was giggling, but as his physician she was serious. "Drink!"

Hotchkins and Tserofed were laughing hysterically.

"Oh, Anuk," Hotchkins said around the laughs, "how bad can it be?"

"Here," Anuk thrust the tube at Hotchkins. "Drink half, then ask me that question."

"Drink!" Mulci insisted while she floated right up to Anuk's face and looked him in the eyes.

"This stuff tastes like a cross between dog piss and formaldehyde! I am not drinking it," he insisted.

Mulci touched a button on her uniform then getting up close and personal she said very seriously, "Drink!"

Two large Fombe wearing what the humans had learned were security uniforms, suddenly appeared at the door to the infirmary.

Hotchkins looked at the two security officers and sized them up. "Anuk my friend," he said with a smile, "I don't think she is going to take 'no' for an answer."

Aboard the shuttle, Anuk and Hotchkins could see the view port up front from their seats. There was not much to see right now.

This was definitely not the shuttle they had arrived on when they came aboard the Ttiflan.

Shiny and polished like new, it was also sleeker and looked somehow more menacing and powerful.

Also in their party were Tserofed, Mulci, and two males named Pomb and Rentahs; which Tserofed described as "Pomb captain Ttiflan. Rentahs captain many ships."

The shuttle rolled down the deck and accelerated. As they cleared the launch bay the two humans were awed by the sights around them.

A ringed gas giant was directly ahead taking up the majority of the view. The rings were clear and distinct. Low and to the right they could see a collection of formations or structures.

But everywhere in the sky, going in all directions, were thousands of ships. They seemed to be all shapes and sizes.

The shuttle nosed down slightly and made another minor adjustment in course. The view of the structures got better. They seemed to be headed toward a large edifice. It was impossible to tell what it was or how big because of the strange construction techniques and nothing familiar to compare it with.

However, something about it gave the impression it was massive.

When Anuk's watch said they had been flying toward this thing for five minutes, it still seemed quite a long way off. But now they could tell. It was a city.

Though nearly covered, you could still spot a few places where the original asteroid showed through.

The city seemed to be built of modular structures. The extremely low gravity of the asteroid had allowed buildings the flexibility to grow both up and out to meet the needs of the occupants. This, without having to be constrained by the heavier degree of gravity such as a planet would produce. If they needed a three-floor conference center added on to the side of a building, they simply added it. This created some interesting if unusual architecture.

They were close now—perhaps half a klick from the nearest building. Occasionally they would see a Fombe near a large view port and could get an idea of the scale.

"Massive," Anuk mumbled. "It must be two klicks tall," he commented on the structure they were passing.

They dodged around one protrusion and the largest structure yet loomed into view ahead of them.

They slowed upon approach and headed for a large gaping maw in the side of the structure. Hundreds of shuttles and small ships were flying in and out of the opening. Soon, their own shuttle was swallowed up by the landing bay entrance. They passed through nearly two kilometers of the structure before making a landing platform.

"Take me to your leader," Hotchkins said as they stepped off the shuttle earning himself an elbow in the ribs from Anuk.

The humans had no more time to investigate the platform as they were hustled into a lift of some kind by several huge and heavily armed Fombe in uniform. Three of the soldiers stood at the door while two searched the occupants of the shuttle.

When they had been cleared the lift proceeded down.

"Down," Anuk thought, "is a barely relevant term in this light gravity."

Eventually the lift slowed and stopped. Then it proceeded sideways at maybe one-tenth G and held that acceleration for several minutes. Eventually it stopped and they were nearly in free fall. They coasted along on inertia for a few more minutes and then braked to a halt.

Throughout the ride in the lift there had been a quiet anxiety among the shuttle passengers. As the door opened, the anxiety increased until it was palpable.

The room they entered was huge. The ceiling was close to forty meters above them. The nearest of the three walls at least twice that. The ceiling was covered with paintings of Fombe in various stages and methods of sexual activity. The walls were covered with murals of Fombe children. Children at play. Children sleeping. Children chanting or singing or any number of other things children do.

The group crossed the room to the far wall where a pair of massive doors guarded the entrance to another room.

The security personnel here thoroughly searched them again, asked Rentahs several questions, and seemed satisfied with his responses. The guard with the most decorations approached the doors, reached out, pressed a stud and a deep gong sounded somewhere on the other side.

Hotchkins and Anuk exchanged nervous glances as the doors started to open.

Hotchkins, using his right hand, made a play gun with it. Pointing the "barrel" at Rentahs' back he said just loud enough for Anuk to hear, "Take me to your leader."

This earned him another elbow in the ribs, but did serve to help ease the tension the two men were experiencing.

The room they entered was half the size of the one they had just exited. It was furnished with sculptures, bas reliefs, paintings, and all manner of art forms, some familiar, some not.

A seawater green carpet ran the length of the room to a Dias. On the Dias was a golden throne complete with jewels encrusted in various places.

A gong sounded twice more and two Fombe came out on the Dias and stood on either side of the throne. The gong sounded again and the two by the throne started repeating some litany in total sync with each other. They continued for nearly ten minutes. Near the end of the litany, the cadence changed and another Fombe came out on the Dias. His outfit was white with black borders. It hugged him closely but was not binding. There was a gold chain with a golden pendant hanging from his neck. On the left breast of his outfit was a picture of the pendant and chain.

He moved with apparent grace in the low gravity. His unhurried manner and sureness of demeanor showed plainly as he took his seat on the throne.

There, he sat quietly until the two Fombe adjacant finished their litany. Then he rose and looked out at the group awaiting his audience and said something the humans could not understand.

Rentahs took a step forward and went into some kind of a speech that lasted about five minutes. When he was finished he stepped back.

The Emperor nodded and sat back down as the other two on the Dias went into a long-winded spiel the humans could not comprehend. They took turns speaking, sometimes for a few seconds each, sometimes for tens of minutes.

Hotchkins was upset when he noticed that this had been going on for two-and-a-half hours. He was getting restless. Edgy.

Finally, they stopped. Then, without a word, the Emperor stood up and walked off the Dias into the rooms in back. The other two Fombe followed close behind.

Hotchkins was pissed. "That's it?" he demanded. "We stand here for nearly three hours and listen to a bunch of garbage and then he just walks out?"

"Hotch," Anuk said seriously, "settle down now. You do not want to irritate the Emperor, remember?"

The others in their party looked distressed at Hotchkins' behavior, but had no idea what to do about it.

Hotchkins struggled to get a hold of himself. The idea of his head rolling across the floor without his body attached seemed all to plausable just now. He used the image to force himself to regain control.

A Fombe came out from one of the side doors to the chamber and went straight to Rentahs. They shared a short and quiet conversation.

At the end of this exchange, Rentahs gathered them all up and they followed the new addition through the side door, down a hall, and into a comfortable looking room. There were pillows, something like a couch but with dividers—which looked remarkably like fold out desks—one large cabinet, and what was obviously a computer system hooked up to an elaborate communications network with a built-in workspace.

The Fombe who had taken the throne earlier walked in rather informally and sat at the computer workstation. He looked at Rentahs with his paired eyes, keeping his center eye focused on the humans, and said something unintelligible. Admiral Rentahs answered in kind and then continued for a good ten minutes.

Hotchkins, impatient as usual, casually reached up and covered his face with his hand thinking, not this crap again. He had not even considered the idea of saying anything out loud before Anuk's arm came around him in a fatherly way and hugged him tightly. A little too tightly.

He turned to Anuk and saw in his friend's eyes more than could be expressed by mere words. For a change, Hotchkins kept his mouth shut.

Finally, the Emperor spoke directly to Mulci. She answered briefly and he responded and stood up.

Mulci turned to the humans and said, "Sit. Drink. Happy time. Learn time."

Tserofed reassured them, "Hotchkins, Anuk friend Fombe. We learn human, you. You learn Fombe, we."

The Emperor went to the cabinet and retrieved several pouches. Floating among the group in the low gravity he distributed them. Plastic tubes of a semi-clear yellow liquid.

The Emperor then joined them among the pillows. Pointing to Tserofed he spoke briefly.

She turned to the humans and informed them, "Fombe Shidig big Captain, hello. Talk, eat, drink, sleep, go crapper. Learn." She finished with a smile. Tearing open her tube of liquid, she took a drink obviously relishing the contents. "Tranja," she grinned.

Hotchkins grinned too, but stopped suddenly when Anuk nearly crushed him in the hug.

"I wonder where she learned that human expression?" Anuk hissed.

"It was a complete misunderstanding, really, Anuk."

"Uh, huh."

A great deal of discussion—with considerable difficulty due to language barriers—followed. They ate, drank, slept when they needed to, and went to what Tserofed insisted was the "crapper," as needed.

Mostly it seemed, they learned about each other.

The Emperor, as it turned out, was named Shidig. He was quite personable. With a quick wit, friendly easy-going manner, and lively sense of humor the humans took to him quite readily.

He also was not an Emperor. They eventually discovered that he was some sort of clan leader that lead not only his own, but all of the Fombe clans. His leadership was based on clan political power, his family's political power, and some kind of voting system the humans could not figure out.

Each clan was made up of many families. The clan that had rescued the two humans was clan Flan. Having discovered the humans seemed to be a great boon for the Flan.

Also, Mulci, Tserofed, and Rentahs gained much personal and family honor through this rescue though seemingly for different reasons. Then, the two men learned that the attack on the Hawking was an act of sabotage by a being of another race called the Binqk. For some unknown reason, the Fombe had a Binqk onboard their ship.

After some discussion about it, and watching recorded images of the incident from several camera angles, the humans became convinced that the Fombe told them the truth. The attack on the Hawking was unintentional.

They also watched recorded images of the battle between the Fombe and the Human ships.

Shidig adjusted the time frame of the images to show the two Fombe ships taking a broadside from the Bismarck, and froze the image.

He turned to Tserofed and said something which she translated as best she could. "Shidig talking, Fombe not fight humans. Humans not fight Fombe, please?"

"You are asking us to stop a war?" Hotchkins stammered.

"Stop fight. Human, Fombe. Stop fight," she said emphatically.

"Anuk, I could use some help here. Just how in the hell do we stop a war?"

"Believe it or not I may actually have an idea on that. Remember when Tserofed told us that the Binqk 'want big fight?' I think they are building up for a war. I am pretty sure now that it was the Binqk that attacked our colony. We may be able to work this to our advantage."

Turning to Tserofed he said, "We need to learn all we can about the Binqk. Talk Binqk. Teach about Binqk," Anuk said pointing at himself.

# CHAPTER 15

DES Bismarck at Space Dock 3, Lunar orbit, Sol system

Seven months after the battle:

The transport pod arrived at one of the docking ports on the Bismarck like any dozens of others each day.

However, when the occupant floated out everyone in view came to attention. A young lieutenant floated up and snapped off a smart salute. "Admiral! We weren't expecting you or we would have prepared a proper greeting."

"At ease, Lieutenant," Admiral Christopher Price raised his voice slightly. "All of you, at ease and resume your duties."

Turning back to the younger officer he asked, "Can you tell me where to find Commander Andreiovich, Lieutenant?"

"One moment, Admiral." Having said that, the Lieutenant walked to a comm panel, pressed a stud, and asked his question. The response was almost immediate. The Lieutenant returned and said, "Commander Andreiovich is in the Weapons Control Center. Do you know the way, Sir?"

"Has it been moved during the refit?"

"No, Sir."

"Then I can find the way. Thank you, Lieutenant."

Admiral Price poked his head into the doorway of the Weapons Control Center for the Bismarck. Inside was a bustle of activity. Several technicians were busy installing or troubleshooting hardware. Some were doing diagnostics on equipment.

One person was cussing loudly. "Dammit, Lois! I said I wanted the targeting systems to be interactive. You told me two days tops. It's been four days. What the hell is going on down there?"

While a voice, presumably belonging to Lois tried to explain, Admiral Price entered the room.

"Alexi! Give poor Lois a break and come walk with me."

"Admiral Price!" Alexi said happily. "Sir, it is good to see you."

Turning to a nearby lieutenant he said, "Roger, take over here. And don't let Lois off of the hook too easily."

"Aye, Sir." The lieutenant responded with a grin.

Floating over to the Admiral, Alexi said, "We were not expecting you, Sir."

"I know Alexi. It's that damn Lao Chin. He has gotten me into the bad habit of doing things informally."

"Then this is an official visit, Sir?" Alexi asked as they floated down the corridor.

"Actually yes. Can we talk in your office?"

"As you wish Admiral," and Alexi took the lead.

Once comfortably settled in Alexi's office, Alexi had presumed the Admiral would inform him as to the purpose of his visit. But the Admiral sat quietly.

After a long uncomfortable silence Price said, "Alexi, why don't you get us both a drink?"

Silently, Commander Alexi Andreiovich opened a cabinet and retrieved two tubes of Irish Whiskey. Wondering what could possibly have caused this somber mood in the Admiral, he floated over and proffered one tube to his superior officer.

Accepting the tube Price said, "Thank you, Alexi." Opening the drink tube he took a long pull of the fiery liquid. "Ah! Now that's the stuff," he said changing his tact. "How is the refit to the Bismarck coming along?"

"Quite well Sir. Oh sure, I give Lois hell. Chief engineers cannot comprehend what anyone says unless every fourth word is a swear word. At that, they take the swearing as approval."

Both men laughed.

Alexi continued, "The new jump drive with the alien-inspired modifications is installed and has passed all of its diagnostics. Our new modifications to the force shields, based on the alien weapons systems, seem to be fully operational. Our previous weapons systems have been updated completely and augmented substantially based on the alien ship's vulnerabilities. They get their first diagnostics tomorrow. We are having some problems with making the weapons targeting systems interactive. Our stellar drive is back up to one hundred percent. We are a good two weeks ahead of schedule."

"That is all good news Alexi." Admiral Price took another pull from his tube of whiskey. "How long till she is ready for space trials?"

"Admiral? Three weeks is the soonest mechanically. But we have not received our new Captain yet. The new skipper will need to be trained and updated on the modifications based on the alien technology."

"You already have your new Captain and I doubt he will need much training on the updates," Admiral Price said earnestly.

"Admiral! My new Captain is onboard and you have not informed me until now?"

"No Alexi. Your new Captain is not onboard. However, the new Captain of the Bismarck is."

"Then," Alexi swallowed a lump in his throat, "I am to be transferred off the Bismarck?"

"No my friend," Admiral Price laughed. "It is with great pleasure and considerable pride that I inform you that you are hereby promoted to the rank of Captain. Along with that promotion, you are ordered and required to take command of the DES Bismarck as of this moment. Congratulations, *Captain* Andreiovich."

"Sir!" Alexi was shocked. "I don't know what to say."

"Well, if I remember correctly, the proper procedure would be for a salute."

"Sir!" Alexi snapped off a smart salute.

"Now Captain," Admiral Price said after returning the salute, "since you are a Captain, and we are in private, please call me Chris."

"Sure, Chris." Alexi smiled and took a large gulp of his whiskey.

"Alexi, we are in quite a spot. This whole alien matter and the CHC situation are entirely mixed up."

"How can that be Chris? I mean we may be going to war with the CHC for a third time, but what could these aliens possibly have to do with it?"

"President Chin has been speaking directly to President McCallister of the CHC. Apparently, she somehow swindled him into a pact in which the CHC and the DES use tension between our peoples to excuse rebuilding the military forces of the entire human race.

"The whole thing is a setup. False press releases of skirmishes—images of minor damage that were not released during the last war."

"To what end Chris? Why, unless they have some reason to think . . ." Alexi's eyes widened. "They expect an attack? Do they have some reason to think one is coming?"

"Alexi, this whole thing of modifying the Bismarck using the alien's technology, has been a matter of testing for precautionary reasons."

"Oh come off it, Chris. I know why the hell we are testing. The precautionary thing has some basis in reality. But, what you are talking about is a whole other ball game. Each half of the human race building up a fleet to fight the other half, but only the leaders know that it is really to fight the aliens? That is one hell of an enormous risk to take. They must have some information—something that they are not telling us."

"They do," Chris rumbled. "The CHC has had three encounters with devices of alien origin that after incursion into normal space, on the edges of a system, have moved in probing the habitable regions of the system. When approached by ships the devices fired at them. Even the lightest settings on a return shot triggered the devices to self-destruct.

"Recently, one of our colonies had an encounter with one of these devices. Only this time, the device malfunctioned upon entry back into normal space. A group of miners accidentally noticed the incursion, saw the device enter normal space, and when they approached it they were not fired upon. They caught it with the grabber arm used to collect small asteroids and brought it back."

"I am surprised it didn't explode if they're designed to self-destruct," Alexi commented. Then he gestured his near empty tube at Chris questioningly as he drifted to the locker for more.

"Bring two more Alexi. And bring one or two for yourself. This may take a while." Stretching out, he yawned, scratched, and waited for the next drink before continuing.

"We got our hands on the thing and studied it thoroughly. Alexi those miners have no idea how lucky they were. Apparently, when the probe entered normal space, some minor disruption during the incursion caused a failure in the sensory system. It was blind. It could not tell that it had been approached or it would have fired on the miners. And those things pack quite a wallop! The damned thing would have wiped out the entire mining ship with just one shot.

"If they had tried to capture the device using any form of energy grappler instead of a mechanical grabber, it would have gone 'boom'!" Chris stopped long enough to take a long pull off his drink before continuing.

"Anyway, our big brains at home back-engineered the programming for the probe. The critters that built it have considerable technology. Most of it far in advance of ours, similar to that of the ship we captured, but not of the same origin. It was as if they were designed by different species at divergent stages of technical evolution.

"According to our computer specialists, they are lousy programmers though. It seems that close to two hundred of the things were mass-programmed at once. All of them were to go to a specific type G star. The specific star was the only thing individual in their programming. They were sent to nearly two hundred type G stars in a region of space basically centered around Sol. They were to look within a specific region—very close to what we consider the habitable region—of the star and search for signs of sapient life. Then, if successful, they were apparently meant to transmit a signal and destroy any guided object approaching within a certain sphere. If unable to destroy, avoid capture by any means. End program."

"My God! They knew exactly which systems and where in them to look for us. How?"

"That we don't know. But according to records of the events, the energy signature of the probe we captured is nearly an exact match for the energy signatures of the ships used in the original attack on the colony we were sent to investigate. It does not however, match the energy signature of the ships that we encountered."

"I don't understand Chris. If the probes match the ships from the original attack . . . ?"

"Alexi, the probes are from the race that committed the original attack. Our best thinkers and scientists believe this means they are definitely preparing for an invasion and a war. Which system it will start in we cannot say."

"But what about the race that we fought? Where do they fit into all of this?" Alexi was trying to get an emotional grasp on this entire situation while remaining externally calm.

"There are several schools of thought on this. Nearly everyone agrees alien race A attacked our colony and destroyed it, so we are at war with A. Then there is a school of thought that says that since alien race B attacked our ship we are at war with them as well. However, there are those who say that since the first two shots at the Hawking were at such a low power setting, they could not possibly be meant as an attack. They had to have been a communication laser. And further, that the high power shot was some kind of an accident making the ensuing battle a colossal misunderstanding. Some think B might be at war with A. Others that B are scavengers following A to salvage whatever they can. Still others have proposed the notion that B are some form of investigators or police.

"In other words," Alexi said, "we don't know squat about them other than the technology we copied from their ship and what we have learned from their deceased crewpersons."

"You grasp the problem precisely."

"So what do you need from me?"

"Alexi, no strike that. Captain Alexi Andreiovich, my friend," Admiral Price began, "we do not know how to find race B. However, we do know how to find race A. One of the other items we gleaned from the programming in their probe was the point of origin.

"Right now we need intelligence. We need a ship to go to the origin point of that probe. And right now, due to her updates and the alien technology added to her databases, the Bismarck is the most technologically advanced ship in the fleet. She has the best and newest state-of-the-art, most powerful, and largest array of weapons now available. Not to mention the strongest armor as well as the most powerful and versatile force screens. Her sensors would be the envy of any science vessel in the fleet."

Admiral Price took another long pull from his tube of whiskey. "She now also possesses the greatest stealth capability of any ship ever built by humans. Captain Andreiovich, I would like you to take the Bismarck to the origin point of that disabled probe. Scout out the neighborhood and learn what you can. Then report back.

"Before you answer Alexi, this is a volunteer only mission. Even for the Captain. We both know this could likely be a suicide mission. You might well make the incursion into normal space and find yourselves looking down the weapon sights of a fleet of alien ships.

"Also, I want you to understand that the promotion is legitimate whether you take the mission or not. If you choose not to take this mission it will be no slight on your record. During the course of this current mission, you will work in the shipyard helping update the rest of the fleet with the alien technology. If the

Bismarck returns, her command is yours if you like. If she does not . . . we will find you another command—a ship of your choosing."

"I must confess to feeling somewhat overwhelmed, Admiral. But I can tell you this: I will *not* turn down this assignment. I am the right man for the job. All of the updates and augmentation due to alien technology have been departmentalized and kept on a 'need to know' basis. There are only two people who know the full story on the upgrades done to this ship, my Chief Engineer Lori Phitz and myself. You need both of us for this mission. No one can claim more experience with these aliens than I can," he continued with a smile. And besides Chris, would you let someone take away your very first mission, on the first day of your new promotion to Captain, and your first day of commanding your first ship?"

"Hell, no!" yelled Christopher Price while holding out his tube of whiskey to drink a toast.

The toast drained both their tubes of whiskey. When they were done with the accolades, Alexi stared at his empty tube in contemplation.

"What is it Alexi?" Chris asked softly.

"Chris," Alexi seemed somber, "I always promised myself that when I finally got my promotion to Captain there were two things I was going to do. First, I would call every damn one of the people I graduated from the academy with and brag. And then I'd go out and get rip snorting drunk—partly in celebration and partly because it would be the last time I could do so—if for no other reason than it would be unseemly for a Captain to be found in such a condition. Now, I cannot call anyone for security reasons. And I dare not get drunk. I know I am going to be up to my brass in mission briefings and getting this ship ready to go," Alexi said.

Chris piped in with, "Those who stand and wait, also serve."

"What in the hell is that supposed to mean?" Alexi asked.

"I have no idea how it relates to the current situation, but it was the only thing I could think of."

Both men got a good laugh from that.

"Chris, about a first officer. I really haven't had a chance to think along those lines, but I really don't see anyone ready to move into that position aboard the Bismarck."

"Actually Alexi, that makes things simpler. Of course, as captain, you are free to choose your own Number One. But I would like to recommend that you consider Commander David Farmer from the Nimitz."

"Oh?" Alexi inquired. "Any special reasons?"

"One or two, maybe three," conceded Chris. "First, he is already involved in this mess. Security clearance for the mission would be no problem.

"Second, he is an outstanding officer who has been held back by being on the wrong ship. With both an admiral and a captain ahead of him, on the Nimitz, he does not stand much chance of promotion.

"Third, and most importantly," continued the Admiral, "he has a great deal he can teach you about fleet movement, fleet control, and fighter command. Conversely, you have a great deal to teach him about command responsibilities from an individual standpoint.

"Alexi, bluntly put, I would like to groom both of you for fleet command. I want you to learn the best points of our new battleships, of which you already have far more insight than any other Captain in the fleet. Plus, I want you to learn how to command an entire fleet."

"Admiral. Sir. Chris. I don't know what to say."

"Alexi, feel free to turn Farmer down. I ask only that you consider him. No matter which way you decide, as Captain of the Bismarck, it is your choice. I still ultimately intend to remove you from command of a single battleship and promote you to command of a carrier fleet. I merely see this as a possible opportunity to kill four birds with one stone."

"Four birds, Admiral?"

"Four birds, Captain! This is how I see it."

"One, David moves to a ship where one way or another he will get the promotion he deserves.

"Two, you benefit from David's training and experience, and move up the promotion's list faster. Thus, opening up a promotion opportunity sooner for David, who has already benefited from your training and experience.

"Three, David, through experience both on the Nimitz and with you on the Bismarck, moves up through the promotion list and gets his own command, be it the Bismarck or another ship.

"Four, David gets command of his own carrier fleet due to both his experience in fleet command while serving on the Nimitz and his experience as Captain of the Bismarck, or whatever ship he ends up commanding.

"So, do me one single favor will you, Alexi?" Admiral Price asked seriously.

"Chris, if I can, it is yours."

"No matter who your Number One is when you leave space dock, bring your ship and crew safely home. I have a hunch there is a whole lot more riding on this mission than either of us realizes just yet."

# CHAPTER 16

Captain Alexi Andreiovich floated onto the bridge of the Bismarck attempting to be casual. The three pips on his collar were still shiny new and quite freshly polished. Pretty much the same could be said about Captain Andreiovich as well. This was only his second week as Captain of the Bismarck—his attempt to be casual was lost, buried beneath the sheer pride and exultation over the recent promotion.

This was also the day they were to launch the newly rebuilt Bismarck.

"Captain on the bridge!" Commander Farmer stated loudly.

"Belay that routine, Mr. Farmer," Andreiovich said. "I expect these people to be able to do their jobs, not snap to attention every time I come to the bridge. But Mr. Farmer! Thank you."

"Sir," Farmer responded simply.

After a review of Commander Farmer's records, Alexi was confident that Farmer was the right man for his Number One. Commander David Farmer had arrived on the Bismarck within seven hours of his decision. The two men had come to know each other rather well over the past two weeks.

Captain Andreiovich had every reason to believe his new first officer would have some passing acquaintance with the alien technology due to his involvement with the aliens. Other than that though, Farmer would need to be trained in the new capabilities of the Bismarck warranted by her updates and upgrades.

As it turned out, Farmer had been part of the team that evaluated the alien technology and suggested how it might be used to augment human ships. Between the two of them they managed to work out most of the problems during the previous twelve days. Most of them.

After three hours of intensive study the two men had concluded that the earliest the Bismarck could launch was eighteen days.

Admiral Price had given them twelve.

Captain Andreiovich looked at his tactical displays and read them aloud.

"Engineering: Both Stellar and Jump engines read one hundred percent. Life Support: One hundred ten percent. Fusion reactors: Reactor Numbers one, three, four, five, and six operating at one hundred percent efficiency. Number two operating at ninety-seven point six percent. Defense Systems: Force Shields at one hundred three percent. Suicide Drones number one through eighty, ready for launch. Board shows green. Anti aircraft systems all read green. Offensive Systems: Missile board shows green for all types of missiles. Railguns show green. Laser Cannons all show green. Particle Ray Cannon, green. Sensors: All sensors operating at one hundred to one hundred thirteen percent of predicted efficiency."

As the Captain of the Bismarck read off the tactical display on his screen, each department head verified the Captain's readings. With no conflicts reported, the Captain turned to his first officer and said, "Take us out of space dock Number One."

"Aye, aye, Sir," responded Farmer. "Disengage external life support."

"Aye, aye, Sir."

"Disengage external power."

"Aye, Sir."

"Disengage docking clamps and moorings."

"Aye, aye, Sir."

"I show all clear of the space dock on my board," Farmer acknowledged. Then, "Aft thrusters at ten percent until clear. Take us out Miss Worthington."

"Aye, aye, Sir!" expounded the woman at the helm.

Alexi Andreiovich could not help but take pride in his crew as each order was carried out with precision.

"Commander, we are clear. Awaiting orders Sir."

Commander Farmer turned to his captain. "Captain, your orders Sir?"

Captain Alexi Andreiovich thought of all the exciting and inspiring first commands and speeches given by all of the Tri-D and old TV captains who had inspired him as a youth.

"One point zero G acceleration to Safe Incursion Distance. At S.I.D. make jump to coordinates in computer file Echo, November, Tango, Echo, Romeo, Papa, Romeo, India, Sierra, Echo. Do you copy?"

"One G to S.I.D., then jump to coordinates in computer file Echo, November, Tango, Echo, Romeo, Papa, Romeo, India, Sierra, Echo, Sir." Commander Farmer barked.

"Very good, Commander. Estimated time to S.I.D. at current acceleration?"

"One moment Sir." Farmer consulted his computer display. "Three hours, seventeen minutes current acceleration, Sir."

"Very good Commander. Once you have us on course and things smooth out, will you join me in my office?"

A smile crossed Farmer's face as he replied, "Aye, Sir."

Twenty-five minutes later the two men were in the Captain's office. "Commander I think we work well together. Your honest opinion?" Andreiovich asked.

"Sir? My opinion should not matter. I am your executive officer. I follow your orders."

"Oh bullshit!" Andreiovich countered. "Any jackass with wealth, political power, or connections can get someone who can say that. I want your opinion."

"Sir, as your first officer I have no complaints. We function well together and I feel confident we can complete this mission if anyone can."

"Christ on a rocket. Get the damn stick out of your ass, Farmer. Either you have been hanging around the brass too much or I have been hanging around President Chin too much."

"Captain?"

"President Lao Chin? You have heard of him?"

"Yes, Sir."

"Well, he has a way about him. Totally informal when he needs . . . Aw, hell," Andreiovich said going to his desk and retrieving two tubes of vodka and grapefruit juice. Tossing one to Farmer he said, "Do you go by David or Dave?"

"Dave is fine, Sir."

"Very well, Dave it is." The captain took a drink before continuing. "First order of business, Dave, is that if you prefer something other than vodka & grapefruit to drink you will need to let me know so I can stash some in here for your convenience.

"Second, I need your honesty. As my Number One, I need, expect, and require you to give me your honest opinions. I will also need your suggestions for alternatives. I do not expect we will always agree, but I want you to feel free to tell me if you don't agree with me and why.

I am not willing to sacrifice military discipline, though. So, if you need to speak in private, we can come into my office. Understood?"

"Perfectly, Sir."

"Good. The coordinates of the system we are jumping to are in the computer file. We know it to be a type G star. That is all we know.

"We believe the race that sent the probes is from that system or has a colony there. I would like your thoughts on how to enter their system and do some intelligence gathering without drawing their attention."

"Normally Captain," Farmer began, "I would say come in high above the ecliptic plane, slow approach under minimum power."

"But not this time?"

"No Sir. Not this time. Since the probes were all launched from that system, it is a good bet the system has a significant industrial base. That being the case, they could well be amassing a fleet in that system which means lots of eyes watching the sky for anything unusual."

"Excuse me," Andreiovich interrupted, "but how do you figure 'it is a good bet' they have an industrial base? Or a fleet for that matter?"

"Sir, it makes no sense to build a fleet of interstellar probes, put them on a ship, and take them to another system to launch. I do not believe they are paranoid enough to do so out of the fear we might find them or they would have made some effort to hide the location of the launch point in the programming of the probes.

"Therefore, I conclude that the probes were built in the system they were launched from. To build two hundred probes of interstellar capability requires a well-established industrial base. Following that line of thought, it would make sense that it is the closest major industrial base to our region of space. Why else build and launch the probes from there? They knew the region of space to look in to find us."

"Given the idea of an industrial base there—and the location is close—it makes perfect sense to amass an attack fleet together at that point.

"However, let us suppose they do not have a fleet amassing there. They still have a significant industrial base and being an interstellar civilization, this implies both local and interstellar traffic and that implies some kind of traffic control system. I would sure hate to get a speeding ticket just before they notify their fleet about us."

A snort erupted from the Captain. "I would hate to get a speeding ticket on the Bismarck's record, too. That was a fine bit of reasoning, Dave. It is almost exactly what the brains in intelligence said in the report I received an hour before we launched."

Taking a drink, he thought seriously about that. "So Dave, what do you suggest we do?"

"Captain, the new jump engines in the Bismarck are far more accurate than those of any ship ever built by human hands. I recommend making the incursion into normal space as close to the sun as possible—far less chance of them detecting our normal space incursion—because there is not much chance they will be staring at the sun. Plus, should we find it necessary to maneuver, there is less chance of anyone noticing the 'tail' from our fusion drive with the sun in the background."

"Very good Dave. Now, dig into our new specs and the star charts. Find out how close to that sun we can safely get. I expect a report in thirty minutes."

"Yes Sir." Farmer was barely out the door when he stuck his head back in. "Tennessee sippin' whiskey."

"Commander?"

"My preference in liquor for the drawer in your desk, Sir." With that Farmer exited quickly, but not so fast he didn't hear his new Captain laugh.

# CHAPTER 17

In a system somewhere along an invisible boarder in space but mapped out between the DES and CHC was a single Red Giant star. If a star could be said to have an emotion, this one would be lonely.

This was a system without planets, without moons, without even asteroids for company. Just a few left over cometary fragments in the outer halo. Currently though, it had two interstellar visitors.

The two ships had appeared on opposite sides of the system. Communications had been established, coded passwords exchanged and verified, and only then did they warily approach one another.

A shuttle departed the CHC Alabama carrying three passengers and proceeded to dock with the second ship.

The passengers were greeted formally, if coolly, then escorted into the presidential suites aboard the DES Starship 1.

"Madam President, welcome." President Lao Chin said by way of greeting.

"Thank you Mr. President. These are Admirals Hurley and Brave Eagle."

"Welcome gentlemen. These are Admirals Price and Wyzincski, and my Science Minister, Habib Assad."

Hands were shaken all around. Nevertheless, the anxiety level was rather high. All four of the Admirals—while never having met—knew of each other thoroughly. They knew their counterparts' reputations, moods, habits, and tactics. They had spent years on opposite sides of some imaginary political line drawn through space defending their own side attacking the other. Point-and-counterpoint.

While they had great respect for their adversary's abilities, they had no respect for their adversary's politics.

Unfortunately for all of them they were caught up in a serious political situation.

"Guard," Lao Chin said to the Marine on duty, "leave us and close the hatch."

"Sir!" snapped the Marine as he made his exit and left the talk to the big mucky-mucks.

Once the hatch was closed and locked the two presidents, four admirals, and the science advisor were alone, President Lao Chin said, "Ally! So nice to finally meet you in person."

"Alright, cut the crap, Lao. You asked for this meeting. Just what is it you need?"

"Ally, I like the way you cut right to the chase, if not the quick," replied Lao. "We are pushing too hard, at least publicly. My top military advisors inform me that our buildup is going well. My information net tells me your military buildup is going well. The problem I have is that my public wants retaliation on a larger scale."

"Whoa," Ally cut in. "Retaliation for what?"

"Therein lies my problem, Ally. The CHC has committed no assault or other activity I can condemn. But the false press releases are getting harder and harder to fake. The people are more and more demanding of retaliation. Madam President and guests, we have a serious problem. I might be able to keep things going just the way they are for maybe another six months—tops."

"So, exactly what is the problem? That the people are unruly?" Allison McCallister asked earnestly.

"Please allow my Minister of Science, Habib Assad, to continue in my place. He can explain the problem better than I."

"Thank you Mr. President." Habib Assad was a rather unassuming fellow. Small of stature, he barely came up to the shoulders of anyone in the room. He constantly gave the impression that he was distinctly uncomfortable in suits. His skin was dark and weather-beaten and his short ebony hair and large bushy beard and mustache were streaked with gray. The wire-rimmed spectacles he wore, perched on the tip of his nose, were strictly for reading. So he was habitually peering over the top of them. The overall effect somehow gave the impression of a man who should be somewhere in the desert at an archeological dig.

"The problem of our individual societies wanting results in a war we are not fighting is becoming more and more difficult. The need for military buildup is getting more and more difficult to explain. The DES and the CHC are nearly built up to the point we had reached at the beginning of our last full scale war.

"If we were truly at war with each other we would have had fleet engagements by now. Our military power on both sides has been built up to such a point. However, we have only been able to show the public minor skirmishes to date. This situation creates three other small problems. One: Explaining why we have had no major engagements. Two: Why has neither side had losses to explain to families and victories to brag of in the press. Three: How can we explain or justify continuing the buildup let alone the cost?

"As I see it, gentlemen and Madam President, we need to fake a major campaign with major losses on both sides."

A round of grumbles and complaints surfaced. Admiral Brave Eagle said, "Oh, please. During the last war we out maneuvered you people at nearly every engagement. That is why we won."

"You were barely able to engage us in battle let alone win a war!" declared Admiral Wyzincski.

For a few seconds, old feelings surfaced and prevailed. President McCallister brought it all to a halt with one shout.

"Enough!" she exclaimed. "We are supposed to be working for the benefit of the human race here not arguing anew our individual political alliances."

"Gentlemen, Madam, if I may continue?" Habib inquired. Taking their collective silence for an affirmative, he forged ahead. "We have a plan to eliminate all three problems. But it requires teamwork and coordinated efforts at the highest levels of our two militaries. It will also involve around one hundred civilians."

Admiral Seamus Hurley looked up. "Civilians? Why?"

"Why? To make a movie Admiral," Assad said with obvious relish at the response he got from his captive audience.

"Movie? What in God's name . . ."

"Have you lost your mind?"

"What?"

McCallister interrupted. "Gentlemen please, let the man talk. I think he just might be on to something here. Please continue Mr. Assad."

"Thank you, Madam President. What we are proposing is to get a movie crew and the best special effects people in the business to create a series of films depicting battles between our two fleets. Then, we report the losses of both ships and crews while actually shipping them off to build up a massive fleet in an uninhabited system."

Seamus Hurley spoke up again. "I can point out one flaw with that plan already, Sir. The fleet we build up in the uninhabited system will be standing watch and waiting. For what, two months, one year? Maybe three years or more? You cannot expect soldiers to sit aboard a ship and play cards that long. We would have massive mutinies on our hands."

Rumbles of assent came from the other admirals.

"Actually, I am glad you brought that up, Admiral Hurley," Assad went on. "We propose that the men build a space station both for fleet support and recreation. In fact, we would also like to build several space docks to update our ships with alien technology after they arrive in the system. That means less cover up of the technology and where it came from."

"Okay then," Lao Chin jumped in. "Can we agree that we have a workable plan?" Murmured assents followed his question. "It seems we have a consensus. So, why don't I get refreshments for everyone and have my chef prepare us something to eat. Then, we can do a bit of good old-fashioned brainstorming and knock some of the rough edges off this plan."

"Just a moment, Mr. President," Admiral Jefferson Brave Eagle said quite seriously. "There is still one major flaw in your plan. How are we ever going to get anyone to believe that even five of your capital ships could manage to destroy just one of our shuttles?"

They all stared at him while he did a count of three in his head. Then a smile split his face and he broke into laughter. The tension in the room disappeared like a fog in a strong wind and the laughter seemed to engulf them all.

# CHAPTER 18

Since their arrival in the Fombe capital city, Anuk and Hotchkins had been guests of Fombe Clan Leader, Shidig.

Shidig's "palace" was part of a gigantic building complex. Both Anuk and Hotchkins found it difficult to get used to the idea that there were no boundaries or signs, nothing to mark where the palace stopped and another part of the multiplex began.

The sections of the building that were not part of Shidig's palace were devoted to various other governmental functions. One of those functions was as an embassy.

Just over five months ago, while touring the embassy, Anuk had spotted an unusual creature. (Funny how you get used to seven-foot-tall, three-eyed people and consider them normal in such a short time.)

The creature was a dark frog-green in color and had six thick stubby legs covered with fine blue hair. Above the forward two legs were two arms with four fingers and two thumbs on each hand. What appeared to be a mouth was located between the two arms. Two necks protruded from the forward part of its back, each containing one large eye.

Curious, Anuk had asked Tserofed what it was. "That is the Pilok ambassador," had been her response. "If you would like to meet him I am sure he would not mind at all. He is quite friendly though he tends to talk a great deal."

Anuk had been introduced to the Pilok ambassador, found him quite personable, and true to Tserofed's warning, very talkative.

The ambassador had introduced Anuk to his entire staff including an engineer named Bakstrah whose job it was to maintain the Pilok technology. (This included one small personal interstellar ship belonging to the ambassador.)

In the intervening months, Bakstrah and Anuk became quite close friends. They spent a great deal of time together comparing technologies and differing techniques of accomplishing given tasks. They also spent a fair amount of time consuming the products of their still.

When Anuk found out the Pilok consumed alcohol, he had spoken to his friend about it. Bakstrah had no method of acquiring the liquid, so Anuk, being the good friend he was, helped Bakstrah design and build a still. It had cemented their friendship.

This time however, Anuk had a different reason to visit his friend.

After a couple of swigs for Anuk and several cups for Bakstrah (Piloks have a much greater tolerance for alcohol) Anuk broached the subject to his buddy. "Bakstrah, my friend, what can you tell me about the Binqk?"

"I can tell you many things about the Binqk. What would you like to know?"

"I have been studying everything the Fombe have on the Binqk. It is a great deal of knowledge indeed: Historical information, economics from four hundred fifty years ago, their religious affiliations, even technical information, and some anatomy. But what I really need is not there."

"And what would that be, Anuk?"

"Everything is over four hundred years old. It seems that the Fombe have no current diplomatic ties with the Binqk. Therefore, they have no current information on Binqk politics."

"Ah," Bakstrah replied. "That would be because most races find it difficult to deal with the Binqk. The Fombe are no exception. From what I recall of my briefing before my assignment to this embassy, the Fombe cut diplomatic ties with the Binqk roughly four hundred and fifty years ago. The Binqk had attempted to sanction the Fombe. They had no trade agreements with the Binqk, therefore they cut diplomatic ties and left the Binqk to their own devices. The Binqk then attempted to drag the Fombe into a war."

"War?" inquired Anuk. "But I thought that with the Galactic Council in control interstellar and inter-species war was impossible."

"Not at all my friend. In fact, the Binqk very nearly succeeded. You see, the more species that join the council, the greater the volume of space needing to be patrolled. The Council is not an entity unto itself. It depends on the member races to uphold its decisions. Council members from the opposite side of the galaxy cannot be expected to intervene in a war that does not effect them."

"I suppose not, but what about those more local?"

"You are worried about the Binqks' current plans to start a war with your people?"

"You know about that?" Anuk got excited.

"I know something of it," answered Bakstrah.

"I need to find out as much about the Binqks' current policies as possible. I am trying to find a way to stop the war before it starts."

"I hate to disappoint you, my good friend, but I doubt you can stop this war. You see, the Binqk have been working on starting a war for nearly one thousand years. It has been a major goal for their race."

"But, why?" queried Anuk.

"For one thing, they are carrion eaters. War creates food for them. Further, war has been their major economic motivator for thousands of years. Since the intervention of the Council, the Binqk have had terrible economic troubles, as well as a major collapse of their primary food supply."

"So they want a war with anyone they can? That just does not make sense."

"The Binqk psyche is difficult to understand. Many races find it impossible to comprehend. My people are some of the few who are willing to deal with the Binqk."

"But," Anuk pressed on, "your people do have diplomatic ties with the Binqk? Do you think there is any way we could find out their plans?"

"Certainly there is. I will speak to the Ambassador. He would most likely find it curious, but would understand why you are taking such a roundabout method of acquiring the information."

"'Roundabout method'?"

"Yes. Worry not, my friend. I will find out what I can for you. Now, if you would be so kind as to refill my cup."

Two days later, Anuk received a message from Bakstrah informing him that the Pilok ambassador would meet with him that evening.

Anuk, Hotchkins, and Tserofed all arrived at the appointed time and place. Bakstrah was there, but no ambassador.

"Bakstrah," Anuk asked, "is the ambassador going to be late?"

"No, friend Anuk. He is not going to be here at all. He gave me the information he acquired and is now attempting to communicate with the Fombe the importance of what he discovered."

"Just a minute," Hotchkins was upset. "Why would he request this meeting and then not show?"

"There is a great deal going on that needs to be discussed with the Fombe clan leader immediately. And, as I said earlier, I have been given the information you requested. Therefore, he went to meet with Shidig while I speak with you."

"Well, then," Anuk said. "What did you find out?"

"It seems the Binqk have maneuvered things quite well for themselves. They have used this opportunity to build up a massive fleet with which to attack your worlds."

"Hold it!" Hotchkins said. "You mean to tell me that the Council is going to let them start a war with us? I thought the Council was formed to deter wars?"

"It was, but your people are not members of the Galactic Council. Therefore, the Binqk have managed to convince them that this is not a matter for the Council to get involved in. "Also, since the 'accident' that caused you and Anuk to become guests of the Fombe, the Binqk are working to drag the Fombe into the war.

"It seems the Fombe executed the Binqk Special Representative after it sabotaged the communications systems and killed the rest of your ship's crew. So the Binqk are working on the Council to allow them to get 'retribution' from the Fombe."

Tserofed interrupted with, "But surely the Council will not allow the Binqk to attack the Fombe?"

"That remains to be seen. The Binqk are working on some secret plan to allow just that. We have not been able to discover what their plan is, but we are attempting to find out."

"Bakstrah," Hotchkins said, "why us?"

"I do not understand the question?"

"I mean why my people, why humans. With a galaxy of beings to fight, why us?"

"Ah," Bakstrah said understanding. "I have taken the liberty to access some of our records on the Binqk that are considerably more up to date than the Fombe records.

"It seems that around five hundred of your years ago, the Binqk found a probe that your ancestors had sent out. It was a very simple device, but it had information inscribed on it as to the parameters of your home solar system. A map, I believe you call it."

"In any case, the Binqk apparently figured you would be an easy conquest and could become slaves and meat food. The Council need never find out until it was far too late to do anything. However, the Binqk discovered your people had advanced incredibly fast technologically. They realized this when they found, and consequently wiped out, your colony on Psht Phas Five. Apparently, when they wiped out the colony and space-based station, they did not know who they had attacked until after the fact."

"Then why attack us at all?" Hotchkins demanded.

"It seems the reason they gave the Council could well have been the truth." Bakstrah mused. "They found a race colonizing a planet that they were ceded by the Council. Also, the offending species was poisoning the atmosphere of the planet."

"My people were *not* 'poisoning' that atmosphere!" Hotchkins stated hotly.

"By Binqk standards you were," Bakstrah stated calmly. "Tell me Hotchkins, why do you wear that device in your breathing holes?"

"So I can breathe. Why the hell else?" Hotchkins rebutted.

"Exactly," countered Bakstrah. "Remember, what you breathe is not what others choose to breathe. By changing the atmosphere into something more suitable to you, you were essentially poisoning it for the Binqk."

Anuk had been quiet and looking quite serious for several minutes. Now he chose to speak.

"We need to get a message to the DES or even better go there and explain it to the proper authorities. We also need to inform the CHC about what is happening."

"What?" Hotchkins asked angrily. "Why warn them?"

"Because, Hotch my old friend, while I have no great love for the CHC either, they are still human. And if that is not good enough, we may need their help for any humans to survive this war as more than 'slaves' or 'meat food'."

# CHAPTER 19

Around a type G-3 star, in an area of space controlled by a race that called themselves the Binqk, there were three planets.

Its close proximity to the sun made the first planet hot. The atmosphere had burned off long ago. Not a large planet and being mineral poor, it had a very low surface gravity—its sole redeeming feature. The low gravity meant that transporting goods and materials to and from factories was relatively inexpensive. Totally inhospitable to life, survival meant living and working in massive domed cities, or in a complete environmental suit.

The second planet was far more hospitable as far as climate went. The atmosphere had needed minor work to make it hospitable. The gravity was nearly a 1.0 on the Binqk scale, and the indigenous animals produced food for all three planets. There were massive food production facilities on the planet plus the normal tourist traps. It was the only facility for a few hundred light years where off duty soldiers could take leave.

The third world was totally inhospitable. Binqk scientists had proven that it would take more time and energy to make the atmosphere breathable than was worth the trouble. However, in spite of its small size, it was fantastically rich in minerals. Due to this fact it was covered with mines, smelters, and any manner of mineral recovery, refining, purification, and blending factories.

Deep down in the system, just barely inside of the sun's corona, a hole in space popped into existence. It went unnoticed, as did the ship that appeared from the vortex. Then the portal disappeared leaving only the ship.

Aboard the DES Bismarck, Captain Alexi Andreiovich turned to his first officer and demanded information. "Report Number One."

Farmer checked his data screen quickly. "Captain, we have made the incursion into normal space exactly where plotted. All operating systems are on full active status. We are operating on passive sensors only, but operating at one hundred one percent predicted efficiency. Full sensors available at your command. Engines all operating well above the norm. No current signs of detection, Sir."

"Very good Number One. But is it just me or is it getting warm in here?"

"One moment Captain. Life support add thirty-five percent more power to your thermal stabilizers," Farmer ordered.

"Aye, Sir," responded the ensign at life support.

"Thank you Mr. Farmer. Science, any signs of detection?"

The lieutenant at the science console double checked the instruments and reported, "Negative Sir. Would you like me to go to full scanning capability Captain?"

"No. Let's be as subtle as possible for a while and see what we find out. We are not in a tremendous hurry to expose our position as of yet. Dammit! It is still getting hotter in here. Mr. Farmer?"

"Life support, add another fifteen percent to the thermal stabilizers. My apologies Captain."

"Mr. Farmer," the Captain asked slowly, "just how close to our safety specs did you bring us in?"

"Sir, you ordered me to plot the incursion into normal space as close to the sun as possible to minimize chance of detection."

"You have not answered my question Commander." The Captain stated quite seriously

"Sir! After plotting the known characteristics of this sun, its diameter and thermal range, we made the incursion into normal space at the maximum safety limits." A half-beat pause and then, "Plus ten percent, Sir."

No one on the bridge actually turned away from their duties but several faces had shocked looks. Two or three actually went pale.

"I see. Very good, continue with passive scanning only. Notify me of anything unusual. I will be in my office." As he floated from the bridge he said, "You have the bridge Number One."

Forty-three minutes later there was a chime at the door to the Captain's office. "Come!" commanded Captain Andreiovich.

Commander David Farmer floated into the cabin. It was clear he was shaken by what he had to report. "Sir," Farmer choked slightly. Then he tried again. "Captain, this is . . ."

"Speak up Dave. What the hell is wrong?" His Captain asked.

"Sir, passive sensors have picked up over ten thousand warships in this system. Not fighters—ten thousand capital ships. Also, nearly seven thousand support ships. There are massive communications to and from all three worlds. The third planet is rich in basic metals and the asteroid belt rich in heavy metals and has a very active mining fleet." Farmer handed the hard copy of the computer data to his superior officer.

Alexi Andreiovich was feeling every bit as overwhelmed as his first officer looked. During the height of both colonial wars, both the DES and CHC together could not have amassed much more than two thousand ships. Now that number was closer to thirteen hundred.

"Dear God!" Alexi mumbled. "This could be the end of the human race."

Then, "Dave, we have to get this information back as soon as possible. Plot a jump but leave it open just a shade. I want to wait another twenty-four hours just to see what else is going on. You never know what might turn up. Notify me immediately if there is the slightest sign of detection. Dismissed!" Then he added as an afterthought, "Oh and Dave, as soon as your duties allow, come back and join me for dinner.

Just over an hour later, Commander Farmer was again admitted into the Captain's office. Grabbing a foothold he caught the plastic pouch Andreiovich tossed to him.

"Thank you Captain." That said, he opened the bag and greedily drank its contents. "Ah, coffee. Just what I needed."

The Captain also opened and drank a pouch of coffee. "Hmm," he mused. "I suppose it does have its merits. But I still prefer vodka," he said with a small wink.

The tension lessened with the humorous banter. But both men were strained from the situation.

"Dave, why the ten percent?" The Captain asked.

"Sir?"

"The ten percent over the safety margins. That was an awfully big chance to take with my ship. Why?"

Farmer was slightly flummoxed at the new direction the conversation took. "Sir, if you are unhappy with the way I have performed my duties in any way why did you invite me here for dinner?"

"At ease, Dave. I never said anything about being pleased or displeased. I asked you a question. I expect your honest answer, that is all."

"Captain, the safety specs were written by engineers who worked on the individual systems. All upgrades were done on a department only, need to know only, basis because of the alien technology. I understood from the overall perspective that with the overlapping abilities of the upgrades we had a minimum thirty-seven percent more safety margin than the specs displayed. I have the computer data available to prove that if you wish, Sir."

"Dammit Dave *at ease*. Truth be told, my data showed a forty-one percent larger safety margin. I only wanted your reasons. I was not questioning your abilities or your actions. Now this is the last time I ever want to tell you this. Get the stick out of your ass! From now on, in my office and only when we are alone, you will refer to me as Alexi. Am I understood?"

"Yes, S . . . Alexi."

"I need trust between us to make this ship run smoothly. That trust has to run both ways. I require the respect due my rank but I hope to *earn* your personal respect. You and I have to work smoothly as a team. And at times, at this level of command, that means putting everything else aside: Anger, jealousy, revenge, hate, personal problems, and being completely honest. If I cannot count on you to answer my questions honestly then this ship could be in danger. There are times when you will have to act as captain because I am unavoidably detained.

"Now, let us drop that subject shall we? Would you like another coffee?"

"Alexi, you have a strange way about you. Maybe it is some of the company you keep."

Andreiovich opened the drawer in his desk and withdrew one more pouch. Tossing it to Farmer he said, "Here you go."

At that point one of the buttons near the collar of the captain's uniform whistled. The uniform was ingeniously designed so that the comm system was actually made of a fiber material and woven into the shirt.

The Captain reached up and touched one of the buttons near his neck. "Andreiovich here," he said simply.

A female voice at the other end responded. "Captain! We have detected a squadron of alien ships headed in our general direction. They are not on an intercept course Sir, but their present course will bring them dangerously close."

"On my way," he said. Then turning to Farmer, "No rest for the weary, Dave. Let's go."

The captain and first officer pushed out of the passageway onto the bridge and floated to their respective command couches where the captain barked a single command, "Report."

The redheaded lieutenant at science station one turned to him and responded, "Captain, we have a squadron of three scout class ships headed this way moving at nearly point-five C. They should pass us at one-ninth AU distance in less than three hours, Sir."

"Thank you, Lieutenant Carey. Recommendations?"

"From me Sir?" Carey stammered.

"You are the most familiar with the situation are you not, Lieutenant?"

"Yes Sir." She looked up at the ceiling as she spoke. "When they pass at apogee it will not be a matter of *if* they can see us, it will be if they are looking our way. At the speed they are moving they have to be doing system patrol, which means they are looking. If we light the stellar engines, the fusion flames would be invisible against the sun but the moving ship won't. And Sir, we were about to inform you, when we detected the alien patrol squadron, that due to a previously undetected quirk in the alien jump technology we cannot create an incursion in the corona. We need to move off to jump."

"It never rains but it pours," said the Captain. "Carey, your recommendation please?"

"Move out quietly so as not to attract attention and make jump, Sir."

"Commander Farmer? Your recommendation?"

"Captain, with the speed those ships are moving they could catch us easily if we move quietly. If we do maximum acceleration out of here we may make the jump before they catch us."

"Number One are you afraid the Bismarck cannot handle three scout ships?"

"Not at all Captain. I simply believe that the message we have to deliver to Earth is so important that it is not worth taking any risks."

Smiling, the captain said, "Thank you for your honesty Number One. With all due respect to the lieutenant here," he said nodding at young Carey, "I think your plan has more merit. Proceed with all due haste please."

"Aye Captain." Farmer said hitting the acceleration warning. "Helm, kick us up to point five gee and then increase acceleration by five percent per second until we reach four gee's acceleration."

"Aye Sir." responded the helmsman.

As acceleration increased, the Captain called out, "Bring all defensive systems online now. We may as well have a good look around. Bring all sensors online and do a full data sweep of as much of this system as you can."

"Captain," called out Carey. "That alien squadron has changed direction and is now on an intercept course with us."

"Bring all weapon systems online. Weapons, I want three missiles with EMP warheads armed and ready for launch. Load all odd rail guns with chaff. Let's see what we can do about jamming any signals from them. We don't want those ships alerting their friends we were here."

Thirty-seven minutes later Lieutenant Carey announced, "Sir, we are now in weapons' range."

The Captain inquired, "Still no sign of a signal from them Lieutenant?"

"None we were unable to jam, Sir."

"Very well. Weapons, Mr. Timmons. I want one of the EMP missiles fired at the lead scout; the other two to detonate same range, fifty klicks opposite sides of the lead ship. On my mark, fire!"

Not waiting for his officers reply, "Fire rail guns one, three, five, and seven at lead ship.

"Time to jump point?"

"One minute fifty-three seconds."

"Captain," Carey jumped in, "one of the enemy has managed to adjust course enough that he might survive the pulse. The other two are too late to miss it. All three are trying to transmit what has to be a warning about us. I believe we have effectively jammed their transmissions, however."

"Weapons," barked the Captain. "Three missiles for our friend out there."

"Aye. Missiles away."

"Lieutenant Carey, I know you are trying but we need to make damn sure those ships do not get any messages out."

"Aye Sir. I report two direct hits on the enemy. One missile destroyed. Enemy vessel appears destroyed, Sir."

"Weapons," The Captain continued without missing a beat. "Treat that ship to another EMP bomb then make sure you run a particle beam over all three ships. We want no survivors telling stories about alien visitors. When you have completed that inform Commander Farmer. We will not jump until you are done. Is that understood?"

"Yes Sir."

"Number One, you have the conn."

"Aye Sir," Farmer responded.

The Captain did not leave the bridge though. Instead, he tied his command terminal into the sensor array and scanned the alien ships as thoroughly as possible.

He did not even look up when the weapons officer reported having completed his task. Not until Commander Farmer gave the command to open an incursion did he look up from his command terminal. Then, seeming distracted, he only stared at the main view screen until they actually entered null space and were safely away.

"Commander," Andreiovich finally said, "at your leisure, will you join me in my office? We have an interesting report to write before we get home."

# CHAPTER 20

The Binqk Emperor was being briefed by its advisors. It was bored and testy, nothing to sink its teeth into here, until . . .

"Liege," Yomin opened, "one of our probes in human space intercepted a public broadcast of great interest."

Pishmah looked up slightly. Yomin noticed and continued. "It seems the humans are divided into two factions. Those factions are currently at war with each other."

Pishmah wriggled with pleasure, "Continue."

"Well, My Liege, it seems that two of their fleets met unexpectedly. In the ensuing battle nearly every ship on each side was destroyed or damaged beyond repair."

"Excellent news, Yomin. Truly excellent."

"Liege, does this mean you believe this to be the time to start our campaign against the humans?"

"No I do not," stated Pishmah. "No, this is a time to use our brains. We will sit back and let the humans fight their war for a while longer. Let them use up ships against themselves instead of us. Those bodies will still be edible when their war ends. Space will guarantee that. It will leave us that many more ships to send against the Fombe."

"My Liege," Admiral Papum said, "I also have a report from the Paastal system. You may remember that is where we have been building up the fleet of ships to attack the humans. Three of our scout ships have been reported missing while patrolling near the solar primary."

"Yes? What happened to them?"

"We don't know, My Liege."

"Well find out. They probably just had too much fermented blood and flew into each other or the primary. Fools, in any case make certain.

"What about our latest operation against the Fombe?" the Emperor continued.

Admiral Eenvupe responded to that question. "My Liege, that operation shall be completed before your next sleep period is over."

"Excellent. Any more good news I hope?" Unfortunately for Pishmah the rest of the session was boring.

Before the end of Emperor Pishmah's next sleep cycle, in a minor solar system controlled by the Binqk, a small tear in space appeared. Out of that tear came a warship. The ship headed directly toward the only inhabited planet and opened fire when it reached weapons' range. It continued the assault until the planet was almost totally lifeless.

The ship that came through the incursion was a Fombe warship. Or rather it had been. She had disappeared approximately fifty years prior and was assumed lost in a jump accident.

Jump accidents were rare, maybe one in fifteen thousand, but they did occur.

In fact, the Wolkacheen had made a successful jump, right into an ion storm. When the storm finished with her, most of the crew was dead. Her life support was destroyed beyond repair. The jump engines might have gotten the remaining crew to safety if they were repaired.

The remainder of the crew had found the jump engines repairable. But sadly, for the want of one small part they did not have and could not create aboard ship, they did not last but a handful of days.

A few small ships, that were local, had chosen to turn their guns on her.

They were like mosquitoes; she brushed them away. She took only minor damage, ignored it, and moved on to the next target: The space-based industry orbiting the devastated planet.

Now there was a swarm of small ships about the Wolkacheen. They were getting bothersome. They managed to cause her damage, but at a horrific price to themselves.

Abruptly, multiple rips or holes in space appeared near the planet. The surviving local traffic authorities nearly befouled themselves believing it to be the remainder of the Fombe fleet. One of them suddenly realized it was the Binqk fleet out on maneuvers and returning at its scheduled time.

The Binqk ships made the incursion into normal space one at a time. As fast as they appeared, they began to receive desperate messages from the bombarded planet and anyone nearby with a communications device. Seeing the destruction they leapt into action.

Hopelessly outnumbered, the Fombe warship, Wolkacheen, was swiftly destroyed. But the ramifications of the attack had been set in motion.

Emperor Pishmah Umselat Bourbaitoo III started out the next day in a much better mood.

# CHAPTER 21

"The Council recognizes Ambassador Mek of the Binqk."

"Gentlebeings. It is with great sadness that I must report to you the blatant attack on one of our worlds. The offending race attacked without warning and without a declaration of war. Nearly fifty thousand of my people were killed in the attack.

"The assailant had just wiped out all the military defenses and was turning its guns on our civilian population, when a small military fleet out on maneuvers made their scheduled arrival in the system.

"Upon seeing the attack in progress, they destroyed the invader.

"We have ample proof of identity from both military and civilian surveillance of the attack and from the fleet that eventually destroyed the invader.

"The race that attacked our colony without provocation and without warning is the same race that, less than one standard galactic year ago, murdered Special Representative Chok, a representative of my government. My government has authorized me to inform you that the Binqk are now at war with the Fombe."

It took several minutes to regain order but the Chairman finally succeeded. "The Council recognizes Brak of the Fombe."

Brak was visibly shaken as he took the podium. Once there, he took time to regain his composure before addressing the Council.

"The Fombe government does not deny executing a *saboteur* aboard a military vessel. Nor do we deny that the saboteur was Binqk. However, we emphatically deny 'murdering' one of your citizens. As for this so-called attack you claim us to be responsible for, I have absolutely no knowledge of it."

"Then you deny responsibility? This is an outrage!" Mek said, turning violet.

"As a representative of the Fombe government, I neither deny nor accept culpability, Ambassador Mek. I stated that I have neither knowledge of the incident nor any reason my people might have to do such a horrific thing. But you stated you have proof. Let us review this proof you *claim* to have. Then I will contact my government and find out what, if any, knowledge they have of this incident."

# CHAPTER 22

It was wartime and all DES forces were at Alert Status One. The war was going badly for the DES. According to official reports, there had been heavy losses and the still powerful CHC might attack any DES planet at any time. All military and civilian watch stations were keeping an eye peeled for any sign of spacial incursions from incoming fleets.

At the outer edge of a system with a sun named Sol and a planet the natives called Earth a hole in space formed.

Several dozen alarms went off throughout the system as soon as the hole appeared. Communications passed the information on to the brass and to other watch stations that an un-scheduled incursion had transpired.

The hole became a tunnel and from this a ship appeared. It settled into normal space and hung there while the hole behind it closed.

Throughout the system there was confusion. This ship was definitely not of DES or CHC origin.

One lone watcher recognized the ship. She kept focused on the area around the newcomer in case of more incursions, while calling directly to President Lao Chin.

Lao Chin took the call, listened, thanked the woman, and hung up.

Then he touched a button on his desk and told his secretary, "Get me Minister Clarke, Minister Assad, and Admiral Price. Immediately! Don't wait for any of them to come here. We will use the Tri-Dee."

"Yes, Sir," the secretary responded.

In the Command Center of the Nimitz, near Lunar Space Dock #3, Admiral Price was receiving reports from several individuals at once. The call from the President was no surprise considering the reports coming in from his staff.

"Greetings Mr. President," Price growled.

"I think you know why I have called." It was not a question.

"Yes Sir," Price responded. "It is definitely the same type of alien ship we fought before. In fact, its markings are identical to the ship that destroyed the Hawking." Price turned to one of his lieutenants. "What?" He demanded.

"Mr. President, I think I had better tie you into this so you can hear it first hand. There is a transmission from the alien ship and it's in English!"

"Yes," the President said, "perhaps you had better."

"This is Engineer First Class Anuk of the late DES Stephan Hawking. DES Service Serial Number 453B1287CB01. I am aboard the Fombe warship Ttiflan. With me is Engineer Second Class Michael Hotchkins of the late DES Stephen Hawking. DES Service Serial Number 187S224EB02, and Admiral Mailiew Rentahs of Clan Flan, of the Fombe Aliance. Admiral Rentahs is authorized to negotiate with the President of the DES.

"The Fombe brought us home to talk and to negotiate peacefully—not to fight or to make war. The previous encounter between Humans and the Fombe was a *tragic* accident, one the Fombe truly regret. Please send an escort to bring us into the system."

Then the message repeated itself.

"Admiral," Lao Chin asked, "have you checked . . ."

"It is coming up on my data terminal now, Sir." Three seconds and an eternity passed before Lao Chin got his answer. "Allah be praised," Price said. "Those are the two missing crewmen from the Stephen Hawking. The Service Serial numbers match!"

"Admiral," began Lao Chin, "escort that ship into lunar orbit immediately. I want no arms displayed when pickup is made. If it is a trap, we are going to fall into it. If what we heard is true this could be our salvation." The newly updated carrier Nimitz, the carrier Enterprise, and the heavy cruiser Prince of Wales met the Ttiflan in the outer regions of the system.

Aboard the Nimitz, Admiral Price was jumpy. "Any new communications yet?"

"Just now Sir. Audio only," the crewman responded.

"On speakers if you would ensign."

"Aye, Sir."

"This is Michael Hotchkins, Engineer Second Class of the late Stephen Hawking. I am aboard the Fombe ship Ttiflan. Are we to be escorted in?"

"This is Admiral Price on the Nimitz. We would like to meet with you face-to-face before escorting you into the system. Security reasons. Do you have access to a shuttle or should I send one over?"

"Admiral, we accept your 'invitation' to come visit. And I for one am grateful. These are nice people but I could sure use a good pizza."

Anuk elbowed Hotchkins in the ribs.

"May we bring two friends?" Anuk interrupted.

"I believe that would be acceptable. Anything else?"

"No Sir. We shall see you shortly."

Anuk, Hotchkins, Tserofed, and Rentahs were transferred via shuttle from the Ttiflan to the Nimitz.

Once aboard, they were inspected, most especially the Fombe, checked for weapons, and rushed to the Admiral's office.

Admiral Price greeted the two humans with profound handshakes. Then he looked at Tserofed and Rentahs, and for a split second was undecided. Finally, he gestured them all to couches.

When they all found a place to sit and then strapped themselves in, he looked at the two humans and said, "You two have had one hell of an adventure. I can honestly say that I am jealous. But tell me about your 'friends' here."

"Our friends Admiral are our teacher/translator Tserofed and Admiral Rentahs," replied Anuk. "Perhaps you would like to ask Tserofed some questions yourself?"

"I have many questions for your friend Tserofed. But at a time when, she?, he?, it?, can understand me," Price said.

"Then please ask your questions, Admiral Price," Tserofed said.

Anuk thought, with a twinge of pride, she hardly has any accent anymore.

Hotchkins would have paid a pretty price to capture the shocked look on Admiral Price's face when Tserofed spoke to him in fluent English. It took several seconds for the Admiral to find his lower jaw and reconnect it with his upper one. When he finally did, he looked directly at Tserofed and asked, "Do you understand me?"

Tserofed replied in perfect English. "Of course I do. Do you not speak English? I have learned English from Anuk and Hotch though I am aware that it is not the only language spoken by your people.

"But forgive me, it has been a long trip. I must go to the crapper. Could you give me directions please?" Tserofed said.

Admiral Price looked like he was about to give birth; Hotchkins and Anuk were in their couches trying to avoid laughing.

Finally, Price regained enough dignity to direct her to the head. Then he said, "Interesting vocabulary she has, gentlemen. I would love to hear all about your adventures. I also know you will tell your tale again and again in the next few days until you are sick of telling it. So, if you prefer, I can wait until we meet with the President to hear your story."

"That is mighty considerate of you, Admiral," Hotchkins replied.

A light came to life on the Admiral's desk and a soft tone sounded. Admiral Price touched a button and said, "Bring it on in Mr. Patton."

Just as Tserofed returned from the head the Admiral's yeoman entered carrying a large pepperoni pizza.

"Since we have a couple of hours to kill before we get to lunar orbit, I thought you might like a bite to eat," Price said.

"Pizza!" Hotchkins exclaimed.

"Tserofed, I have no idea what your people eat but we can find something for you and Admiral Rentahs if we know your dietary requirements and preferences."

"Thank you Admiral Price," Tserofed replied. "Hotch has told me a great deal about pizza and it smells so good. I would like to try it."

She turned and asked Rentahs a question, received an answer, and said, "Admiral Rentahs is intrigued with the smell. He would like to try pizza also."

The two aliens were delighted with the pizza and the small group made quick work of it.

Then alarms started ringing. Admiral Price touched a button on his shirt and said, "Price here. Report!"

"Admiral," came the voice at the other end. "We have another unscheduled incursion happening."

"On my way," Price said. "Would you folks come with me? I have a sneaking suspicion this is going to involve you."

The Admiral rushed through the hatchway to the bridge followed closely by Anuk, Hotchkins, Tserofed, Rentahs, and one security escort.

"Report!" barked Price.

"Sir, we have another unscheduled incursion occurring. Location is fifteen hundred kilometers off Lunar Space Dock #3," the lieutenant reported.

"Can you tell how many ships are coming through?" Price asked.

"It appears to be only one ship Sir. One moment. It's the Bismarck, Admiral."

"Well, it appears we have ourselves a reunion," Admiral Price muttered.

# CHAPTER 23

Admiral Hurley had taken a shuttle to his cruiser hidden in the rings of Saturn. From there he was returning to bring the latest news and the Fombe proposal to President McCallister of the CHC.

Tserofed and Rentahs had returned to the Ttiflan for a sleep cycle. Anuk and Hotchkins were given temporary quarters aboard Starship 1. Before retiring to their quarters though, they requested an audience with the President, Admiral Price, and Minister Assad.

The meeting took place in the President's office. Once they were all seated, Lao Chin turned to Anuk and Hotchkins and said, "Well gentlemen, you obviously have something on your minds. Would you care to enlighten us?"

Anuk started, "Mr. President there are a few things we did not mention earlier that you should be aware of."

"While the Fombe and/or Admiral Hurley are not present, I take it."

"Yes Sir." Anuk continued. "We both had time to learn quite a bit about the alien technology. We have some ideas to improve weapons systems, power systems, and propulsion systems for both stellar drives and jump engines."

"Just a moment," interrupted Minister Assad. "You may not be aware that we captured one of the Fombe ships during the battle in which the Hawking was destroyed. I doubt there is very much about their technology you could teach us now that we have had a chance to take their ship apart and study it."

"Minister, that might be true about Fombe technology but the Pilok are far more advanced in weapons technology. Also, their designs for communications systems are radically different and far superior. I believe we could adapt both for our cyberfighters."

"Whoa. Hold your horses. The Pilok? Who the hell are they?" Price demanded.

"Another alien race, Admiral," Hotchkins jumped in.

"Mr. President, Admiral, Minister, I spent a great deal of time with a Pilok engineer," said Anuk. "We mostly discussed alternative approaches to different technical problems. As it turns out, the Pilok were quite eager to share. They are adamantly against this war the Binqk have started. Their political position is that they will not get involved in an armed conflict unless they are attacked first. However, they are willing to help by providing intelligence and technical information."

"One moment please. It looks like this is going to be another long discussion." Tapping a button on his desk, President Lao Chin said, "Gerry better bring another pot of coffee." Turning back he continued, "Do go on, please."

"Well Mr. President, the Pilok have diplomatic relations with both the Binqk and the Fombe. They have offered to provide us with intelligence on the Binqk."

"And how do we know they will follow through with those promises?" Habib asked.

"Because they sent my engineer friend Bakstrah along with us to help with technical innovations. That, and they sent along data that spans several hundred years of recent history and trade information about the Binqk. In addition, troop and ship movements for the last year and a half."

"I must see this data!" Habib stated excitedly. "Mr. President we can analyze this data for weaknesses and strategies."

"Admiral," said the President, "maybe we ought to call a break until we get Andreiovich, Farmer, and this 'Bakstrah' here with 'his, her, its?' data on the Binqk."

"Yes, I agree Mr. President. But I have to ask you, Anuk. How did they get information on recent troop movements?" Chris Price queried.

"I asked Bakstrah the same thing," Anuk replied. "Do you know what he told me? 'We asked'."

Just over two hours later all of the humans had arrived for the conference and the only "persons" not present were Admiral Rentahs, Tserofed, and Bakstrah.

Conversation came to an abrupt halt as first the two Fombe entered and then Bakstrah. Everyone but Anuk, that is.

"Bakstrah! Welcome my friend." Anuk proceeded to make introductions around the room with Bakstrah in tow.

"Good Lord!" Admiral Price whispered quietly. "Three-eyed bipeds are one thing but that bugger isn't even vaguely humanoid."

"Nothing says all intelligent life must be bipedal Chris. We probably seem rather strange to him. Possibly ugly, too," whispered Habib in return.

As introductions got around to Habib, Bakstrah said, "It is pleasant to meet you Minister Habib Assad. And thank you for defending the appearance of my race."

Anuk had not heard the whispered comment so he quickly continued "Admiral Christopher Price."

"Admiral Price." Bakstrah pronounced the English words amazingly well and moved his eyestalks wide apart while leaning in close and showing his teeth. He uttered softly, "If you do not care for my non humanoid appearance, perhaps I should just eat you for my evening meal!"

Several people around the room had shocked looks on their faces at Bakstrah's words. None more so than Admiral Price.

Knowing Piloks were almost totally vegetarian, Anuk had a huge grin on his face. It didn't stop him however, from hitting Bakstrah with a right jab that would have dropped any human to the floor. Even in this one-tenth gravity environment Bakstrah barely budged.

"Bakstrah!" Anuk raised his voice, "quit pulling the man's leg. I am sorry, Admiral, Bakstrah can be a royal pain in the lower extremities of the back. He has a twisted sense of humor."

Admiral Price did not even look at Anuk. Instead, he leaned in closer to Bakstrah. His eyes narrow, glaring, and cold. Then, baring his own teeth, he growled, "I have killed and eaten bigger game than you. And you would make an interesting looking meal on a chafing dish with an apple in your mouth."

The two stared hard at each other for a few short seconds that seemed an eternity to everyone else in the room. Abruptly, Price broke into a smile and laughing punched Bakstrah in the same manner as Anuk had. Bakstrah also broke into a laugh that sounded all too human and gave Admiral Price a playful tap that sent the man tumbling across the room.

After this playful exchange the tension settled down and several conversations started happening at once.

Habib was questioning Bakstrah. "So, instead we use your 'magnetic lens' to focus the laser? Ingenious! But how to keep the heat within a safe range is going to be the major obstacle."

"Not at all," Bakstrah said. "Our thermal capacitor can hold a great deal of heat until you get the chance to release it safely. Or release it slowly to generate extra power for the ship."

Hotchkins was speaking to Commander Farmer and Captain Andreiovich. "If we could integrate the Pilok's communication technology with our cyber technology, it would drop the response lag time dramatically. At least fifty percent from what Anuk and I figured."

"Listen, the technology may work but with our power systems?" Farmer put in. "Especially since we built this combined fleet with power systems bastardized from Fombe technology."

"We have got to try Dave!" Captain Andreiovich expounded. "If we can make it work we can add, by my calculations, nearly half an AU range to the fighters without increasing response lag time."

"Yes Admiral!" Anuk was saying. "That's one of the beautiful things about Fombe jump engines! You can reach a destination and not make the incursion into normal space immediately. You just sit in Null space until the time you choose to make the incursion.

"That way a support fleet could go to a particular location, send a scout ship into normal space without risking the entire fleet, and wait for the 'all clear' before re-entering normal space again. This would leave little or no need for supply fleet protection and leaving more ships free for duty on the lines."

Admiral Rentahs and President Chin were conversing with Tserofed acting as translator. "So," Lao was saying, "you will keep us informed of what the Binqk are doing through the Pilok Ambassador's connections. We will build nothing but carriers and cyberfighters from here on out. You will send us as many fighter pilots as you can for now, while looking for volunteers from your fleets to train as cyber pilots. We send some of our experts on cyber technology to help your people integrate our cyberfighter technology into your ships' systems. The Fombe Alliance, the Democratic Earth Societies, and presumably the Confederated Human Colonies declare an alliance and mutual defense pact against the Binqk.

"Quite correct Mr. President. This alliance will also include the trade of goods, services, and technologies among all of our peoples," Rentahs responded through Tserofed.

"Excellent Admiral Rentahs. Please allow me to contact my counterpart in the CHC so that she might come here, see your evidence, and hear your offer for herself. But I suspect she will agree."

"Thank you, Mr. President. May your bed be always warm and full."

"Now, if you will excuse me while I make the call." Lao excused himself and left the room to call President Allison McCallister.

Once in his office, he sat at his desk for a few seconds to compose himself before actually making the call.

Allison McCallister had obviously been woken up. She looked tired and haggard. "Yes Lao, what is it?"

"Ally, Seamus is on his way with extremely delicate information for you. Some things have happened since he left. I am not at liberty to discuss it—even over a secure channel. But, when he arrives it is vitally important that you return with him immediately. You might want to bring your science advisor and someone who understands cyber technology."

"Lao, you do know what time schedule I'm on, right? What the hell is this all about?" she asked, no longer looking or acting the least bit sleepy.

"What it is about is that you need to take whatever precautions you deem necessary to feel safe, but when Hurley arrives you need to get your buns to the Sol system A.S.A.P.!"

"Right, well if it is that important perhaps I had better not wait for Hurley to arrive. I am on my ship now and we can depart within the hour. I will leave a message for Hurley to make the turnaround when he arrives and have my advisors gathered and waiting to return with him. Will that suffice?" Allison inquired.

"Completely, I owe you dinner and drinks for this."

"Shows what you know," she quipped. "You owe me a night of dancing as well."

President Allison McCallister closed the communications with President Lao Chin. She sat a moment and pondered. *What made me agree so easily? Certainly there has officially been war between our peoples. But that is a hoax and I know it. Yes, we had actually been at war just over eighteen months ago. But Lao and I have built up a working relationship, a trust between us since then. And why am I even thinking about this? Am I really such a pushover? Am I that lonely at the top? Is it because he is my only political equal?* She flushed red with embarrassment, as she tried to figure it out.

Eventually, she decided it was the sincerity in his voice that had convinced her. Having come to that conclusion, she tapped a button on her desk. The first mate had the bridge watch and appeared on her monitor. "Yes, Madam President?"

"Mister Weems, would you please wake up the Captain and inform him I need to get to the Sol system immediately. Tell him to have someone contact me one half hour before we make the incursion into normal space." She disconnected without waiting for a response.

Then she called her aide. "Yes?" A bleary-eyed woman of oriental ancestry answered.

"Sing, please round up a pot of strong coffee for me. And you had better bring me a sandwich too. Make it ham and Swiss on rye with extra mayo if you can. And some fries with extra salt and lots of ketchup.

"Yes Madam," came the response.

That taken care of she started making calls to Vice President Leo Walsh, Minister of Science Arnold Sebut, and Admiral Brave Eagle.

She had just finished her call to Vice President Walsh and was talking to Minister Sebut, whose bleary eyes had nothing to do with lack of sleep. He had been celebrating at his daughter's wedding with a bit too much champagne. "No, no!" she was saying, "I need you to come now! If you are not capable of understanding that simple order perhaps I should send a couple of Marines to escort you. In fact, stay where you are. Do not leave the reception I will send an escort for you."

"Thank you, Madam President. I appreciate that courtesy," Sebut said with a slight slur in his voice.

She disconnected, placed her head in her hands, and closed her eyes for a few seconds.

That was when Sing came in carrying a tray. She set it down and with a flourish pulled the napkin off the top revealing the contents.

The President lifted her head to look at the food on the tray. "What is this, Sing?"

"Shrimp salad. Orange slices dipped in honey. Graham crackers with peanut butter. One cup of coffee and a pot of herbal tea," Sing said quite calmly.

"I know that, except about the herbal tea in the pot that is. What I meant was that this is not what I ordered. I specifically ordered ham and Swiss cheese on rye with fries and coffee."

"Yes Madam, you did. However, you have gained two more pounds and we need to watch your waistline. Furthermore, you have a bad habit of eating poorly. I believe we have discussed your eating habits before." In point of fact it had been discussed many times over the years they had worked together. A conversation they seemed to have more and more often as the years passed. "This meal is far healthier."

"But," replied the President, "it is *not* what I ordered."

"That is correct, Madam President," Sing smiled at her.

"You know, technically I could have you flogged for this," the President quipped.

"That tradition applies to ancient sea-going naval vessels, Madam," Sing replied totally unruffled.

"A Navy is a Navy whether it is on the sea or in space. And a tradition is a tradition," President McCallister stated firmly.

"I will grant you the Navy is still the Navy, and traditions have a way of standing, Madam. However this vessel, while government owned, is not technically part of the Navy. Therefore your argument is moot. May I be of any more immediate service, Madam?"

"Not if you won't get me any real food," the President grumbled.

She was shoving a bite of salad into her mouth and setting up the connection for Admiral Brave Eagle as Sing exited the room.

# CHAPTER 24

$S$omewhere in the Sol system in an orbit near Saturn, DES Starship 1 forged through the night. In the President's office, deep in her armored belly, President Lao Chin was presiding over a meeting.

"Ladies and Gentlemen," President Chin said changing the subject. "One minor problem we have failed to consider with everything else going on is what to do about Anuk and Hotchkins."

"How do you mean, Sir?" asked Minister of Foreign Relations Mandy Frost.

"Case in point Mandy," President Chin continued. "How much do you know about the Fombe? Do you speak their language? Do you understand their body language? Can you tell me about their political structure?"

"Well no, I don't know much about the Fombe. So? What do you expect, we just met them," Mandy Frost stated defensively.

"Relax, Mandy. I didn't mean to put you on the defensive. It's just that we do have two humans who speak Fombe, understand their body language, and their political structure. They also know a great deal about their technology."

"Mr. President what is your point?" inquired Habib.

"My point is, to send them back to simple engineering duties would be a waste of manpower and material. I would like them both promoted to the rank of Lieutenant Commander. Hotchkins has good rapport with the Fombe. I would like to appoint him as their Ambassador. Anuk has an excellent relationship with the Pilok—appoint him Ambassador to them.

"Since both also have a great deal of knowledge of their respective alien technologies, I further suggest we appoint them Joint Ministers' of Alien Technologies."

When no one else broke the uncomfortable silence Captain Andreiovich finally said, "Excuse me, but am I the only one who has had the time to read these men's service records? They are not exactly academy material you know."

Admiral Price started reciting from memory. "Hotchkins, Engineer Second Class, has been busted in rank twice and pay once. He's been arrested three times for drunk and disorderly while off duty and spent a total of six months in the brig. It has cost him promotions at least three times. He has an IQ of 190 and an incredible talent for engineering principles. According to all his academy instructors and commanders he has a deep disrespect for authority, which sporadically gets him into trouble.

"Before his transfer to the Hawking he worked on two carriers during the last war and a cruiser during the previous one. I can sum up the gist of what every commander has said about him by quoting just one: "Hotchkins dislikes authority and refuses to show proper military respect. But when a ship's system or a cyberfighter is down and needs immediate repair, he is the man to have on the job. His mechanical and engineering skills are unsurpassed and under pressure he is unerringly reliable."

"Anuk, Engineer First Class," Price continued after half a beat, "busted in rank once because he disagreed with his chief engineer's assessment of the ship's engine status during a battle situation. He was certain the engines would blow if stressed. The chief attempted to tell the captain it was safe to go ahead and Anuk knocked out five of his teeth in one punch. His actions ultimately saved the ship and crew. He was correct and the chief was wrong. He has been reduced in pay five times for operating a still aboard ship. Three of those times it was so well disguised that it took an explosion from CHC weapons' fire to blow up the still. The device was not discovered until an investigation after the fact. His IQ is rated at two hundred and three. Anuk holds Ph.D's in Theoretical Physics and Quantum Mechanics. He has written two papers on jump technology, that were ultimately used to design the most recent non-alien inspired updates for our jump engines. He has turned down two offers to teach physics, quantum mechanics, and engineering at the academy. His reason, he claims, is that 'A good engineer should not be afraid get his hands dirty'."

"I have been thinking about the same problem Mr. President," Captain Andreiovich commented dryly.

"I would say you have considerable reason to question their appointments Captain," Minister Clarke said. "Are these really the men you want as our alien ambassadors, Mr. President? As Ministers of Alien Technologies I can understand why you would want them, quirks and all, but they are not exactly model citizens now, are they?"

Habib Assad jumped into the conversation. "Bob, I suspect if we looked close enough we could find skeletons in everyone's closet. At least with these two men everything is out in the open."

Minister Clarke's thoughts quickly flashed to a scandal with two underage girls that had been quickly hushed up and he immediately dropped his argument.

Let us face the facts, gentlemen," said President Chin. "These men, warts and all, have already developed an excellent rapport with the aliens. They stopped a potential war between humans and the Fombe. They turned the Fombe into an ally and brought us another potential ally in the Pilok. They also have managed to secure information on our race's newest and most dangerous enemy, the Binqk. Information which we had absolutely no other means to acquire. They brought back technical advancements that we are only beginning to understand. They have opened trade negotiations with the Fombe and potentially with the Pilok. All of this, in just over one year.

"I would have to say that they have already done pretty well as ambassadors for the human race. Why not let them *officially* continue the job they started?" he concluded.

"I have to admit," Mandy Frost chuckled, "those two have accomplished more in the last year, as far as foreign relations go, than I have in the last seven. And I have been working with humans," she added with a snort and a toss of her hair.

"Any other comments?" the President asked.

Minister Clarke looked perturbed but said nothing. Captain Andreiovich seemed uncomfortable with the situation but kept silent as well.

"Alright then, it is settled. They are both to be promoted to Lieutenant Commander and made Ambassadors as well as joint Ministers of Alien Technologies.

"Admiral Price will you take care of the military promotions please?"

"Of course Mr. President."

"Now," Lao Chin said changing the subject again, "what are we going to do about letting the public know we have made alien contact and are at war with an alien race? I need some ideas people."

"Mr. President," Minister Assad started in, "we cannot just 'let the public know' this right now. Too much mental shock and we could have rioting on our hands. I believe it would be prudent to begin a propaganda campaign and gradually ease their minds into the idea of alien contact . . . over a period of months."

"Provided the Binqk allow us that kind of time," Admiral Price put in.

"If the Binqk attack, nothing we do with a propaganda campaign will make a damn bit of difference," Assad countered. "If they hold off for a while we may need to be careful about how we inform the public."

The discussion continued for three more pots of coffee and several more hours.

# CHAPTER 25

Resident Allison McCallister of the Confederated Human Colonies had just floated out of the sonic shower and donned her robe when her desk in the next room started to chime.

She floated carefully out of camera pickup and activated the connection.

"Yes?" she inquired.

"Madam President," the Captain replied, "you requested to be notified one half hour before the incursion into normal space."

"Thank you Captain. Once we arrive in normal space please send my regards to President Chin. His ship should be in one of the pre-addressed orbits near Saturn."

"Yes Madam. Will that be all?"

"Yes, thank you Captain," she said disconnecting the link.

Ally finished dressing and "made herself presentable" in time for the incursion into normal space.

She was seated at her desk when it chimed again.

"Yes?"

"President Chin sends his regards and asks us to rendezvous with his ship as soon as possible," the Captain stated flatly.

"Thank you Captain. Please proceed with the rendezvous and have my shuttle ready when we arrive."

"Yes, Madam President," came the response.

As she closed the connection she wondered at the captain's calm reaction to her orders. Certainly he knew there was no conflict between the CHC and the DES. Still, less than two years ago, the two great human societies had been at war. The captain's primary responsibility was to keep her safe at all times. And now here they were entering the home system of the DES without so much as one escort ship.

A smile crossed her face as she thought he must be ready to rip his hair out about now. Yet, he remains as outwardly calm as if they were merely showing tourists around the home system.

The acceleration warning blared briefly then slowly weight started to return. In a matter of five minutes it was at 1.37 standard gravities and holding. This was the gravity of the planet Allison McCallister had grown up on—standard policy to make acceleration equal to the gravity on the current president's home planet.

They had barely reached the full one point three seven G's of acceleration when there was a knock that interrupted her thoughts. "Come," came her simple response.

Sing entered with a tray of food, which she set down on the desk. "What now, Sing? Oatmeal with fruit, a side of dry wheat toast and milk?"

In response, Sing removed the napkin covering the food. "Ham, eggs—sunny side up, toast with real butter and fizzle berry jelly, apple Danish, orange juice, and a large mug of espresso. There is more espresso ready to brew in case you want seconds," Sing recited.

"Real food, Sing? Has my physician told you that I am dying or some such? Or has there been some kind of mistake?" the President teased.

"Madam President," Sing stated firmly, "you are about to go confer with the President of the Democratic Earth Societies on issues that could affect the entire human race. It would not do to have you functioning at anything less than one hundred percent capacity because you had a sour stomach from your breakfast or were grumpy about what you were served. Therefore, this is a logical as well as practical choice.

"Your concern for me is touching," the President said with a note of both sincere affection and sarcasm.

Sing's response was serene, "Thank you Madam. If you excuse me I will return in a few minutes to see if you need anything else."

After being excused, Sing casually left the room to check the cornbread in the oven. Making sure the door was securely closed, she continued on until she was out of sight of the two well-armed marines guarding the door. Once no one could see her, she allowed herself a well-earned smile.

For the second time in a matter of months the two ships, carrying the two most powerful people in human space, made rendezvous.

Communications were established and permissions granted, so the newly arrived ship sent a shuttle across to the other waiting vessel.

The shuttle docked with DES Starship 1 without incident.

Thanking her pilot, President Allison McCallister opened the shuttle's door and extended the ramp herself rather than waiting for an aide to do so.

"Welcome aboard Madam President," President Lao Chin said warmly.

"Thank you, Mr. President. Now that we have extended formalities, let us get straight to business. You had urgent need to speak with me in person as quickly as possible."

"Of course, Madam. Would you please accompany me to my office?"

Once inside with the door securely closed, he turned and spoke. "Ally, my apologies for the mystery. However, as you will remember from the briefs about our encounter with the alien fleet, when the Hawking was recovered two of the bodies were never located?"

"Yes, vaguely. Why?"

"Well, we found them," said Lao Chin. "Ally you might want to sit down."

Puzzled, McCallister sank into a chair. "What do you mean 'we found them'?"

"They were actually taken aboard the alien ship during the battle. They have been living with the Fombe for the past year. The Fombe are the alien species we captured the ship from. This is all very complicated and it might be best if I just give a synopsis of the events to bring you up to date. I am sure the majority of the details can wait until your staff arrives. It will take quite a while to cover all of the details of events, so it does not seem to make much sense to explain everything twice."

"Very well Lao," Ally replied graciously, "but at least continue with the synopsis. You have certainly got my attention. So, as long as we are waiting, have you got any good coffee?"

# CHAPTER 26

During the nearly nine hours of President Chin's synopsis of the situation, the two Presidents ordered snacks twice and consumed nearly three pots of coffee. President McCallister tentatively agreed with Chin on the decisions he had made regarding the Fombe/human alliance pending her own Cabinet's approval, of which she felt rather certain.

They finally reached a point however, where President McCallister felt totally overwhelmed. She turned to President Chin and asked, "Do you think I might meet with these Fombe now so that I might get a feel for them for myself? I believe I have reached the information saturation point anyway."

"Certainly Ally. The hour or so of transit from their ship would also give us both a much needed break."

"Wonderful. Then if you don't mind," she reached to touch a button on her blouse.

"No, not at all," Chin answered.

Touching the button she said, "Sing would you please bring us the bottle of flavodka now?"

"Of course, Madam President," came the response.

"Flavodka?" Lao Chin asked inquisitively.

"A specialty of my home world. When my ancestors first colonized my home planet they planted, among other things, potatoes. Of all the Earth plants cultivated, this strange thing happened only to the potatoes. A native bacteria somehow 'merged' with the potatoes and created a new species. A potato with a very strong spicy flavor, non-toxic, but delicious. We call them spicetatoes.

"Of course, someone had to try making vodka with them. It turned out that they made a mash and a mighty fine wine. But you cannot distill it because it is too flammable. The result of the mash or wine mix was flavodka, because the discoverer really wanted vodka. It is a spicy mildly alcoholic drink, with the added effect of a natural stimulant. Between the low alcohol content and the natural stimulant it is nearly impossible to get drunk. But it does create an interesting 'heightened awareness.' I brought along a very rare bottle thinking perhaps you might like to try some."

"I am not sure how comfortable I am with the 'heightened awareness' part of that," Lao Chin responded.

"I can certainly understand your concern your never having experienced flavodka," Allison answered seriously. "However, I plan to consume a small amount myself even if you do not. Do you truly believe I would consume anything that might possibly inhibit my mental capacity just before I meet with the Fombe delegates for the first time?"

"It hardly seems likely," Lao commented.

There was a knock on the cabin's hatch and President Chin called, "Enter."

Sing crossed the threshold carrying a silver tray with a bottle and two glasses. "Where would you like this, Madam President?"

"The coffee table will be fine Sing, thank you," Allison said. Then she turned to Lao saying, "Besides, Sing would never allow me to consume anything deleterious before an important meeting. She mother-hens me half to death as it is."

"What Madam President means," Sing replied placidly, "is that I take proper care of her." Changing the subject she continued, "Mr. President, I have consulted with your aide Gerry and we both feel it is time the two of you ate a complete meal. You have consumed nothing but snacks for several hours. Would you care to dine now, Sir? Madam?"

"Do you see what I mean, henpecked?" Allison quipped.

Lao Chin joined in the game. "Oh yes, I see it clearly."

"Dinner will be served in one half hour, Madam President, Mr. President." With that, Sing exited the cabin.

"You know," Lao Chin stated flatly, "I don't recall either of us actually saying we wanted dinner right now. You may really be henpecked, Ally."

Lao Chin marveled at the sweet and spicy flavor of the flavodka and after a small glass realized what Allison meant by heightened awareness.

Lao had allowed himself a second small glass before their dinner arrived—Allison had three glasses in the same amount of time.

"Ally," Lao said, "I feel like my mind is clearer than it has been in years. Is that the flavodka?"

"I'd like to believe it's my perfume, but yes it is the effects of the flavodka."

Lao Chin caught the implications of her statement but before he could respond there was a knock on the cabin hatch. Lao called out, "Come."

Sing entered carrying a large serving tray. Right on her heels was Gerry laden with a large platter.

Sing and Gerry moved together in a harmony of service. It was almost as if the whole routine had been rehearsed. Each action and every motion was carried out with maximum efficiency and minimum effort. A veritable ballet of choreographic service.

Dinner was delicacies from half a dozen worlds in each of the two great societies.

Scampi, abalone, cricketodile legs, baked slamon, tourt fish, deerhog steaks, and meanfrog from DES worlds.

Cloudbread with fizzleberry jam, scrimps in hampai sauce, baked fecklesquash, moonberry torts, skyteaser breasts, sweet gahk, and spicetatoes from CHC worlds.

No sooner had they finished when Sing and Gerry reappeared, as if by magic, bringing espressos and removing the dishes and leftovers. Again, they worked together in perfect harmony and seemed to waste not one single motion.

As Lao and Allison sat down on the couch with pouches of coffee, Lao turned to Allison and said, "Ally, I feel it fair to warn you that the appearance of these aliens is somewhat disquieting."

"Oh come now, Lao. I am not a squeamish schoolgirl. I am nearly eighty-five standard years old. I don't think three-eyed aliens will shock me."

"I thought the same thing before I met them. But, it is one thing to intellectualize aliens. It is another to meet them face-to-face, especially Bakstrah."

"The Pilok?" Allison inquired. "You never did tell me what they look like."

"Yes, the Pilok. Well they should be here in a few minutes. Maybe you should wait and see for yourself."

"Very well," said Allison. "But fair warning. This dinner was provided by both of us and therefore does not get you out of your debt of dinner and drinks. Let alone a night of dancing."

"Point taken and understood," Lao acknowledged.

The two sat back sipping their tubes of espresso in a total, though comfortable, silence.

It was Lao who finally broke the stillness. "Ally, I have to wonder. As politicians we need to be able to keep quite a few eggs in the air at any given time. But, I keep asking myself, even with our combined talents and the overwhelming desire to protect the entire human race, if we could be juggling too many eggs? Could this whole thing come crashing down around us at any second?"

"Of course it could," she replied. "To deny the possibility would be ludicrous. But do I think it will? I don't know Lao. I just do not know. We can only do what we feel is right for the survival of our species. We must combine our respective factions. Right now I think we stand a good chance of pulling this off, in large part thanks to you."

There was another knock at the cabin hatch. "Thanks Ally," Lao said softly, then louder, "Come."

Ambassador Anuk and Ambassador Hotchkins were practically strutting around in their brand new uniforms. The pips on their collars declared the rank of Lieutenant Commander, so new, they glistened in the artificial light. The ambassadorial insignia on the breast of their jackets was as new as the pips. Both men were feeling very smug and extremely pleased with themselves.

When the call from President Chin came though, they wasted no time. Gathering up Tserofed, Rentahs, and Bakstrah they took a shuttle to DES Starship 1.

Anuk was slightly irritated that he was not allowed to pilot the shuttle himself. During the year with these aliens he had not been able to fly anything because Fombe ships were not designed to be piloted by the much shorter humans.

Now he was informed that it was beneath his rank to fly his own shuttle. His irritation was short lived however. They were on their way to meet with the two most powerful humans in the galaxy.

At his knock on the hatch to the President's office, Anuk heard President Chin call out, "Come."

Even as the door opened and they started through, Bakstrah became interested in the weapons carried by the marines guarding the door and asked to see one of them.

Anuk entered, followed by Hotchkins, then Rentahs and Tserofed.

"Gentlemen!" President Chin greeted them. "Do come in please."

As introductions were made, Anuk noticed that President McCallister seemed somewhat preoccupied by the two Fombe.

"President Allison McCallister, this is Admiral Mailiew Rentahs of Clan Flan, of the Fombe Alliance," President Chin was saying.

Anuk smiled to himself as he noticed President McCallister's response to the aliens. She paled visibly, her eyes dilating. But her voice was rock steady as she said, "Admiral Rentahs, I am pleased to meet you. It is my sincere hope that what you and President Chin have started here can be continued beyond the DES and carry over to the CHC and the entire human race."

Tserofed translated the greeting and then the Admiral's response. "Admiral Rentahs is pleased to make your acquaintance. He also wishes for this to be a fruitful beginning for both of our peoples."

President Chin turned to Anuk and said not quite accusingly, "It was my impression that Bakstrah was coming to this meeting."

"Yes Sir," Anuk responded. "He is outside the compartment door talking to one of the marines. He was fascinated by the weapon and wanted to see one."

"Good luck to him," Chin snorted. "Those guards will not even let me get one out of their hands to look at."

Another knock at the hatch and Bakstrah entered the compartment. Allison McCallister had been chatting with Rentahs but turned to meet the Pilok.

She took one look at Bakstrah and her eyes grew wide, her knees weak. Had there been gravity, she would have had to sit down before she collapsed onto the couch.

"God in Heaven!" squeaked out from her open mouth.

A grin splitting his face, President Chin said to her, "President McCallister, may I present Bakstrah of the Pilok."

Bakstrah came over, reached out with his right hand and said, "Very nice to make your acquaintance, Madam President."

Unsure of what to say or do, she finally reached out and shook Bakstrah's proffered hand.

"You speak English?" She managed to say.

"Yes, Madam President. Anuk has taught me some of your English language and taken the time to learn some of mine."

"Yes, well," President McCallister stammered. "That will simplify things considerably."

President Chin jumped into the conversation with, "Gentlemen, Tserofed, Madam President may I offer any of you some refreshments?"

The humans and Bakstrah all decided upon flavodka. The Fombe found the odor disgusting and settled for mint tea.

They spent the next three hours just getting to know one another and exchanging information. The Fombe played the vids of Binqk Special Representative Chok sabotaging the Ttiflan's communications system and the replacement of the damaged equipment. They discussed the Binqk's plan for war with the humans and the Fombe, the Human/Fombe Alliance, and how they could best work together to get ready for the Binqk attack.

Suddenly, there was a rude sound from Bakstrah. They all turned to look at him. "Excuse me please," he apologized, his eyestalks turning a darker green than usual. "It must have been the flavodka."

All at once, President Chin got a strange look on his face. Making a comment to himself, he hurried to a wall panel and turned the environmental controls to full in an attempt to clear the air in the room.

Various groans and complaints were voiced rather loudly before they finally decided it was time to postpone the meeting long enough to move to another compartment.

# CHAPTER 27

Emperor Pishmah Umselat Bourbaitoo III was absolutely furious. A state of mind that was extremely dangerous to those within close proximity. "Admiral Eenvupe, the First Fleet is in place to attack the Fombe. Why are we not ready to attack the humans yet?"

"My Liege," Eenvupe chose its words very carefully. "Many of the ships are still in need of repair. An unfortunate leftover effect from our previous emperor and his civil wars. Our shipyards are doing repairs as quickly as they can. The workers are doing double shifts in an attempt to complete repairs on the fleet. Also, many of our ships are still in need of fuel, munitions, and troop replacement. The workers on the munitions ships are working as fast as they can to replenish supplies, but there is a great deal of work still to be done before we are ready to attack."

Pishmah screeched in a fit of rage, drew its sidearm and shot one of the slaves cowering at its feet. "Admiral Eenvupe you will give me a time estimate until the fleet is ready to make the attack," Pishmah raged. "And Admiral, you had best be accurate. I am not in the mood to tolerate disappointments just now."

Eenvupe did some rapid calculations before responding. "My liege, I estimate three months time need pass before we will be ready to make the assault upon the humans."

Then, in an attempt to change the subject, Eenvupe added, "Have you chosen the first system we are to attack, my Liege?"

"Very well Admiral Eenvupe," Pishmah said in a dangerously calm tone. "Three months. At three months and one day, if we are not ready to make the assault on the first of the human worlds you will be aging meat for my meal." Then, allowing the change of subject, "Yes, I have made my decision." Pressing a button on the control panel built into its throne it brought up a three-dimensional hologram of star charts.

Systems known to be occupied by humans were highlighted in blue. Using the controls in its throne, the Emperor focused the chart in on one of the blue highlighted systems. "We will begin our assault here. It appears to be the capital world of one of the human factions. By destroying it, we will disrupt their seat of government making it easier to conquer the other worlds occupied by this faction."

"An excellent plan my Liege." Eenvupe responded with more enthusiasm than it felt.

Pishmah turned its attention, "Admiral Papum, is the Second Fleet ready to start the assault on the Fombe?"

"My Liege," Papum responded nervously, "the same problems restrain the Second Fleet as restrain the First Fleet. Many ships are in need of repair, munitions, fuel, and even troops."

"And how soon will the Second Fleet be ready to make the assault, Admiral Papum?" The dangerous tone was again in Pishmah's voice.

"The Second Fleet is spread over several systems my Liege. This has the bonus of multiple shipyards to do the work of repairs and munitions replacements. However, at present, the First Fleet has been given priority for munitions and troop replacements.

"As things stand, I estimate it will be four months before the Second Fleet will be ready. Of course if you make the Second Fleet priority, the First Fleet will not be ready within the time frame allotted, my Liege."

"Are you recommending that I make First Fleet priority over the Second Fleet, Admiral?"

"No my Liege. It would be foolish for me to second guess your plans when all can see your wisdom in this matter has been proven true and just."

"Well said, Admiral Papum. We will proceed as I have planned. The First Fleet has re-supply priority. Once we have crippled the human resistance capabilities, we will deal with the Fombe."

# CHAPTER 28

$L$ao Chin was a young child again, laughing and playing in the lagoon in front of his family's estate. The warm water caressed his body and buoyed him to the surface. Dolphins swam with him and chittered their own laughter as he splashed about.

But something was wrong. Lao Chin was not able to identify what it was. It seemed to be lurking in the shadows of the deep parts of the lagoon. Something he could not quite see but could definitely feel. A presence, ominous, dangerous, and definitely overwhelming.

Something that seemed to be coming specifically for him.

He turned to swim towards shore and safety. But now the current was taking him out to the depths where the dangerous thing lurked. The harder he struggled to swim toward shore, the stronger the current taking him away became. He swam for the shore with every bit of energy he had, but to no avail. The current was just too strong.

Now that dark ominous thing was coming up to get him. He was panicked and swimming for his life. It came closer and closer.

It reached out for him, to drag him under to the depths and away from the life giving air he desperately needed. Just as it touched his foot, an alarm sounded somewhere on the shore.

President Lao Chin sat bolt upright in bed. Covered with a cold sweat and shaking nervously, he realized that the chiming was not an alarm but a request from the communications officer.

Taking a few seconds to gather his thoughts and shake off the residual effects of his dream, he finally responded with a voice-only circuit. "Yes?"

"My apologies Mr. President, but I have Ambassador Anuk on hold for you Sir. He says it is urgent."

"Very well. Put it through to my desk, will you?"

Slipping on his robe, he made his way to his desk in the next room. He had no sooner sat down when a knock came on the cabin door.

"Come," he called.

Gerry came in still in his bathrobe, but carrying coffee in a refillable pouch, which he set down on the desk. Then he quickly left without a word.

Lao had a stray thought about how Gerry could have known, but dismissed it as something best left unanswered.

Picking up the tube of coffee and taking a sip, he activated the connection to the incoming communication with his other hand. Anuk's face immediately appeared on the screen. It seemed drawn and haggard.

"Anuk! You look terrible. So, I assume this is not a social call?"

"No Sir. Though I must say, Mr. President, you do not look to be in the best of health either."

"Yes, well, we all have our crosses to bear. Why have you called?"

"Mr. President, I am afraid I have some troubling news. Since the Binqk declaration of war against the Fombe, the Galactic Council has chosen not to interfere due to the purported attack by the Fombe against a Binqk world.

"Further, the Galactic Council seems to be coming apart at the seams. With the Council's decision to not get involved in the war between the Fombe and the Binqk, several other races in various areas of the galaxy have taken the opportunity to declare war on each other.

"Now it appears that the Council cannot control the outbreak of wars. Therefore Sir, we cannot count on any help from the Council. We humans on our own against the Binqk."

The President took a deep breath and let it out slowly before responding. "Understood, is there anything else?"

"Yes Sir," Anuk replied. "The Binqk have set the time and location for their first attack on us. In eighty-four days the Binqk fleet will launch an attack on 4725 Cancri, the seat of the CHC government."

"Dear God," President Chin said. "Anuk, how reliable is this information? I mean is it authentic enough that we can depend on it with a reasonable amount of certainty?"

"It comes straight from the Binqk Ambassador to the Pilok. This ambassador is not noted for being brilliant, apparently. It was bragging to the Pilok Ambassador about the plans during a state of intoxication. This was also independently verified by other means I dare not mention over subspace radio, even a secure communiqué. Suffice it to say that the Binqk may be familiar with sabotage and subterfuge, but not espionage."

"Understood," said the President. "I will pass this along to President McCallister. Anything else?"

"No Mr. President. Except that perhaps you should try to get more sleep, Sir."

President Chin gave a snort at that. "Yes, well, I will do what I can. Thank you, Ambassador Anuk," President Chin said as he closed the connection.

Lao Chin went into his bedroom to get dressed. As he did so he gave thought to his next move.

Allison, Seamus, Alexi, Chris, and Bob Clarke all needed to know immediately of this new information.

Going back to his office he started to sit down at his desk to make calls only to find breakfast waiting. Gerry, he thought. Maybe it was time to find out how Gerry seemed to know what was going on even before he did.

# CHAPTER 29

The Fombe cruiser Ttiflan was docked at the Fombe military space habitat designated Foos-Chay Pount. Roughly translated it meant Repair and Preparation Facility 42—a full military ship support facility complete with space docks, machine shops, electrical shops, foundry, and production facilities.

On the tiny flight deck of the Ttiflan a project was under way. A project involving two humans, one Pilok, and a score of Fombe.

"Dammit!" Hotchkins swore from the underside of the fighter they were working on. "I can't get to the damn connection to check it. One lousy connection is holding up the whole test. Shit!"

"Relax Hotch. We are not even sure that it is a bad connection," Anuk added calmly.

"Well if it isn't, it's back to the drawing board and two weeks worth of work down the damn drain." Hotchkins turned and hollered to the Ttiflan's chief science officer, "Skarl, we're going to need a lift here so I can get underneath this bird and check it out. Shit!"

"Hold your elephants, stay where you are, and shut your basta for a moment Hotch." That said, Bakstrah walked around to the front of the fighter and using both hands carefully lifted the nose of the three-ton mass a good two feet.

"Can you reach it now, Hotch?" Bakstrah said with a slight grunt.

"Jesus Christ on a rocket!" Hotchkins mumbled. Then louder, "Yes I can, but can you hold it up long enough to allow me a good look?"

"Yes," Bakstrah informed him, his face turning a darker shade of green "if you quit wasting so much time swearing and check the damn thing."

Hotchkins fumbled around under the fighter for a couple minutes.

Anuk was getting worried as he noted Bakstrah turning an even darker green and around his eyestalks he was starting to twitch. Just as Anuk was about to say something, Hotchkins rolled out from under the fighter. Quickly he said, "Okay Bakstrah I'm out. You can set it down now."

With a groan, Bakstrah set the fighter's nose carefully back on the deck. "Well?" he demanded of Hotchkins.

"I think we got it this time folks. I did find a bad connection and I fixed it."

"Excellent," Skarl replied. Then she tapped the comm unit on her wrist and said, "Try it now Meestar."

In response, the fighter craft's reaction thrusters started to gyrate on their own.

Meestar, the test pilot for the prototype Fombe cyberfighter, did not need a call on the comm unit to know the problem had been fixed. He could hear cheering from all the way across the landing bay.

The odd assemblage of beings were all very excited to have the fighter responding correctly. The combination of human, Fombe, and Pilok technology had presented some challenges, but they seemed to have overcome them all. The only thing left to do was a test flight.

"Let's get that baby ready to fly," Hotchkins cheered.

"Not so fast you two," came a voice from behind him.

Hotchkins and Anuk both turned to find Mulci standing there looking irritated.

"Neither of you has slept in nearly two of your days. And neither of you has eaten in at least eighteen of your hours. As your physician, I order you both to go take a meal, a shower, and a nap. Then, you can continue with the tests."

"Now just a damn minute!" Hotchkins started.

"Hotch," Anuk said loud enough to stop the argument before it got started, "for once in your life, shut up. I can handle this."

With that, Anuk took Mulci by the arm, gently turned her around, and started walking. "Mulci," he started, "you are right of course. But we are at a crucial stage of this project."

"You say that every time I suggest rest, Anuk."

"True enough. But remember, the whole project is crucial to both of our survival," he countered. "So how about a small compromise? We get the fighter launched for its test flight. While it undergoes the first phase of tests we grab a bite to eat. Then, as it makes its way across the system in a series of distance tests, we get a nap in. Will that fill your prescription?"

"Very well," Mulci grumbled. "I suppose I should feel lucky that I didn't have to call security to enforce that much of my prescription."

"Mulci," Anuk said excitedly, "you're beautiful when you're angry." He gave her a kiss on the cheek then quickly turned back to the business of getting the fighter launched. Mulci stopped him saying, "I am beautiful all the time, you just never noticed!"

The group watched the fighter go through its first series of tests while munching on what the Fombe called sandwiches. Hotchkins grumbled that they were not sandwiches because, "This is not bread." Though it did not stop him from devouring the food.

The fighter had completed its first series of tests and was headed across the system when a chime sounded in the flight center. Skarl, being the closest, pressed the button to respond. "Yes?" she inquired.

The Ttiflan's communications officer responded with, "I have a call for Ambassador Anuk from President Chin."

Anuk leaned over and spoke to the panel, "Pipe it down here will you please?"

"Sir?" The communications officer was confused by the idiom.

"I would like to take the call down here if you can arrange it."

"Yes. of course, Mr. Ambassador."

Anuk grimaced slightly. Proud as he was of this new title, it took quite a bit of getting used to. Though it was not much better, he felt far more at ease with his other newly added title: Joint Minister of Alien Technologies. At least 'Joint Minister of Alien Technologies' sounded like something an engineer might aspire to.

The screen in front of the small group came alive with the face of President Lao Chin.

"Gentle beings," President Chin greeted the group. "I called expecting to speak to Ambassador Anuk. But this is also quite satisfactory. How goes the business of modernizing the Fombe fighters?"

"Mr. President, you look like you finally got some sleep, Sir. Mulci's counterpart must have enforced the prescription," Anuk laughed.

"As a matter of fact she didn't," Chin laughed. "I just plain fell asleep and none of my staff chose to wake me."

"I see. We have just launched the first of the Fombe cyberfighters and completed its initial series of tests. At present we are waiting for it to cross the system to perform the second series of tests. The long range trials." Anuk answered.

President Chin looked stunned at the statement. "You *just* launched the first of them for a test? We only have five more weeks until the Binqk attack is supposed to take place. How can you possibly get enough of their fighters ready in such a short time?"

"Mr. President," Hotchkins jumped into the conversation, "we merely had to work out the details and bugs of combining human, Fombe, and Pilok technology. Assuming this test goes as well as planned—and so far it has exceeded our hopes—we should be able to make four to five conversions per day with just our team. And we have three other teams working with us, studying our data, and learning what we are doing and why.

We are streaming live broadcasts of what we do with full technical specs to other ships and shops all over the Fombe Alliance. Don't worry, Mr. President. If the Binqk allow us the five weeks projected, we will be ready in time."

"That is excellent news, gentlemen. Truly excellent. Admiral Price informs me the Fombe pilots being trained here are working out superbly. In fact, we have had to quit production of carriers temporarily so that we could reassign the workers to building fighters in order to produce enough cyberfighters to keep the Fombe pilots supplied. That means we will have roughly four thousand additional cyberfighters. Admiral Price and Admiral Hurley are both in agreement that we stand a fair chance of winning the first engagement and causing a devastating blow to the Binqk military. That is, if our intelligence on their attack plans is as accurate as believed."

"Let us hope, Sir," Hotchkins replied seriously, "that it will be enough to make them think twice before attacking us again."

"Mr. President," Anuk interrupted, "I am sure you called for more than a progress report on how we are doing."

"You are, of course, correct Ambassador. I must ask once again. Is there no way that the Pilok would come into this fight on our side? In spite of all this good news, we could still use the help."

Bakstrah stepped into the pickup to speak to the President. "Mr. President, I must reiterate. My government is quite firm about this. Unless we are attacked first, we can do nothing more than provide technical advice, information on the Binqk, and logistical support. We cannot and will not get involved in any physical conflict until that time."

"Until that time?" President Chin queried.

"Yes Sir." Bakstrah provided. "My government's best scientists have projected a ninety-seven point six percent chance that we will be drawn into the war by a series of attacks coming from the Binqk Empire."

"But, if you are that certain the Binqk will attack you eventually . . ." President Chin supplied.

"Even while there is only a two point four percent chance we will not be drawn into the war, my government will hope for that two point four percent," Bakstrah stated. "Mr. President, we Pilok take contracts and treaties very, very seriously. At present, Sir, we have a non-aggression treaty with the Binqk. Until and unless they break that treaty, my government will not become involved in this war. Truth be told, Mr. President, I have been surprised that my government has allowed me to provide you with as much data and technology as they have."

"Bakstrah," President Chin stated seriously, "on behalf of the Democratic Earth Societies and the Confederated Human Colonies we are sincerely grateful for what you personally, and your government as a whole, have done to help us. And you have my personal gratitude as well. When the opportunity presents itself please forward my gratitude to your government. And if you would, further inform them that on behalf of the DES I would like to open official diplomatic relations and trade with your people. I also believe I can reasonably say that the same goes for the CHC."

"Mr. President, I am sure I can say on behalf of my government we would welcome such relations. While we do have diplomatic ties with the Binqk they are, to say the least, strained. Was there anything more you need to discuss with either Anuk or Hotchkins Mr. President?"

"No, thank you Bakstrah. I believe we have covered it all for now."

"Then I bid you a goodbye, Mr. President." Bakstrah said as he closed the channel.

# CHAPTER 30

Deep in the center of the Binqk Empire, within a military fortress that served as the Emperor's Palace, Emperor Pishmah Umselat Bourbaitoo III was regaling the Royal Court with its plans. "This will prove to be a great new age for all Binqk everywhere. Early this morning, on my personal orders, we launched a fleet of eight thousand war ships to attack the humans. The human system I chose for our initial attack contains the capital world of one of the two human factions. The overwhelming force my plan brings to bear, should be able to totally wipe out all human life in that system. This will disrupt the government of that faction to the point that they will never be able to coordinate their forces enough to bring significant military force to bear against us. Then, with that faction's government rendered powerless, we will next attack the other faction's home world and create the same impotence there. The humans will never get the opportunity to bring more than a handful of ships to bear against our fleet of nearly eight thousand war ships."

"Attacking at the same time will be a fleet of nearly three thousand warships launched against the Fombe home world. Our estimates of the Fombe military capabilities show this to slightly exceed the maximum number of ships they can put into action at any given time. Thus, delivering a decisive blow to the Fombe at the same time we deliver our first decisive blow to the humans."

All of those present wriggled with delight. Even the slaves were happy with the news. New slaves meant less work for all. Besides, even slaves have a pecking order. And new slaves were on the very bottom of the list.

Anuk, a Lt. Commander in the Democratic Earth Societies Navy, Ambassador to the Pilok, and Joint Minister of Alien Technologies had just finished a twenty hour shift refitting Fombe fighters to be cyberfighters. Filthy, hungry, and tired he had decided to take care of the problems in that order. A long hot shower helped ease some of the tension in his aching back as well as washing away a layer of grime. He had almost finished toweling off when the Ttiflan's alarms started sounding. Almost immediately, a call came to the desk in his cabin where it kept chiming for a response. Wrapping a towel around himself he touched the button to activate the call. "Yes?" he inquired.

A recorded image of Admiral Rentahs spoke to him, "Anuk, please come to the bridge as quickly as possible. We have detected hundreds of incursions forming. Rentahs out."

Anuk dressed hurriedly and dashed to the bridge of the Ttiflan. There, he looked at the view screen with its tactical printouts and realized how serious this situation truly was.

Rentahs turned to him and said, "They are Binqk war ships. We have counted over one thousand and the incursions are still happening."

"Admiral, what is the status of your ships and fleet?" Anuk asked in a cold tone.

"Four hundred thirty seven carriers converted to fly cyberfighters. Just under a thousand capital ships, around one hundred thousand fighters, and thirty seven thousand cyberfighters scattered across the system."

"Admiral," Anuk said politely, "they have us outnumbered three to one with capital ships and they are still coming through. I find it easy to believe they can match us, or very nearly so, in fighters."

"I feel the warmth of your reasoning. The Binqk though, generally are not so dependent on fighters. They depend more on what your people would call a battleship. However, you will always learn when you try a new branch of the tree. You have an idea?" Rentahs hoped.

"Sir," Anuk began, "our only real advantage is the cyberfighters. Launch one third of the cyberfighters we have on an intercept course with the Binqk fleet. But do not perform any high gravity maneuvers. Approach at normal fighter acceleration."

"What good will that do?" Rentahs queried. "They will just launch their own fighters to intercept ours and a long bloody fighter battle will ensue."

"Not exactly Admiral," Anuk stated. "When they approach weapons range, our fighters accelerate to maximum and punch their way through the Binqk fighters and head for the fleet. The Binqk fighters should follow them to protect their capital ships. Then you launch the second third of cyberfighters. Full acceleration until they hit the Binqk fighters in the rear. Effectively this places the Binqk between our forces. Then, when our fighters break through theirs and wipe out the threat of Binqk fighters, launch the final third equipped with torpedoes. Recall the first two waves of fighters to refuel and rearm, then go attack the Binqk fleet with our armada of capital ships right behind."

"An excellent plan. However, I have been reading some of your history from the memory chips your president gave me. One of your greatest military minds once said: 'Even the best battle plan cannot survive contact with the enemy,' Napoleon Bonaparte."

"It was just an idea Admiral," Anuk shrugged.

"But a good one." Turning, Rentahs spoke to his crew, "Communications, patch me into all military channels system wide."

"At your discretion, Admiral," the communications officer said.

"This is Admiral Mailliew Rentahs of Clan Flan. A Binqk war fleet is currently entering the system. All stations to Alert Status 1. This is no drill.

"All ship-based fighters to launch immediately. All station-based fighters are to stand by. I repeat, all ship-based fighters to launch immediately. All station-based fighters are to stand by."

Cutting the broadcast with a gesture to his Communications officer, Rentahs turned to Captain Pomb. "Captain, please plot a rendezvous for our cyberfighters and send them on an intercept course with the Binqk fleet. Then plot a rendezvous for our fleet and issue the orders.

# CHAPTER 31

Wing Commander Pleethka had been chosen to transmit battle data directly to the Emperor due to a combination of being the best orator amongst the few available, and being the second best fighter pilot in the entire Binqk fleet.

The best pilot in the fleet was a lousy orator and was handed the ignominious position of flying cover for Pleethka.

The ten next best fighter pilots were all in Pleethka's squadron. The Emperor hated disappointments.

Pleethka had just been confirmed a link directly to the Hall of Audiences and the Binqk Emperor, and was starting to make its report.

"The fighters have all made our rendezvous and are moving to intercept the Fombe fighters. I find my squadron at the spearhead of this action, a great honor indeed.

"The Fombe fighters have shown no sign of backing down from the fight even though we have them outnumbered better than two to one.

"Their capital ships appear to be moving to engage us. Perhaps they will be easier meat than anticipated. We have their capital ships outnumbered three to one.

"We are coming into weapons range. All weapons systems online. Inertia compensators online."

"My Liege," interrupted Yomin by way of explanation, "the inertia compensators are a new innovation to our fighters that allow our pilots to pull tighter turns and sharper maneuvers."

"So they nullify the effects of inertia?" asked the Emperor.

"Not exactly My Liege. But they do allow our pilots to pull an extra two gravities unimpaired. We feel this will make a big difference against our opponents."

Pleethka had finished its checklist and was back to reporting what was happening. "We are almost within weapons range and the Fombe show no sign of turning or breaking ranks. I am engaging weapons lock on the lead Fombe fighter. Almost . . . almost . . . Fresh meat! Where did they go? Behind us? Impossible! No ship could maneuver like tha . . ."

Nothing but static followed this transmission. The Emperor's entire entourage was outraged. The Palace Communications Specialist on duty was nearly was put to death in the few minutes it took to locate another transmission from the fleet in the Fombe home system.

" . . . repeat. This is Admiral Papum. The Fombe have beaten off our attack force. They have some kind of fighter that does not seem to adhere to the laws of physics, inertia, or kinetic energy. I cannot explain it. I am transmitting the scans of our attack and the response of their fighters. A great many Binqk have died here today to provide our Emperor with this very expensive data. My Liege, make good use of it. I cannot make the jump home and expect destruction shortly. The same can be said for the few ships remaining in my command. We pledge our lives to our Emperor! Again, I repeat. This is Admiral Papum. The Fombe have . . ." A loud explosive noise and the "whoosh" of escaping air, then only static from the other end.

Emperor Pishmah wailed its rage aloud. It thrashed about and beat its appendages on anything handy. It found a laser pistol kept hidden in the folds of its couch. Before it settled down, three slaves and one courtesan lay dead. None of the remaining guests, courtesans, or slaves dared make a sound or move abruptly lest they attract the Emperor's attention. Survival instincts took over until the Emperor showed very unmistakable signs of having settled down.

This did not happen until the report came through that it was time for the First Fleet to start the assault on the human world.

Common sense, plus the "advice" of one of the members of the High Court, accompanied by a rather nasty looking pistol shoved into a vital area, caused the Palace Communications Officer to make sure that the only link to the system the humans called 4725 Cancri, was through Admiral Eenvupe, Commander of the Imperial First Fleet.

# CHAPTER 32

T here is a white F2 star the early settlers in the system designated 4725 Cancri, named from an old cult television show, several TV offshoots, and a dozen movies that ran from the 1960's through the 2030's.

The only habitable world—Memory Beta, the seventh planet—is home to the Confederated Human Colonies.

All traffic control, watch stations, and military posts had been on high alert for three days in a row.

Aboard space station Lagrange Five, Chief Katy O'Shea was starting her shift watching the sensor scopes. The standing order as she took her station was: "Code red one status. Be on highest alert. Attack imminent."

Strangely enough the attack was supposed to be from an alien race and not the DES.

That in itself had convinced quite a few of her comrades in arms that this was all some sort of a drill. The only thing happening out of the ordinary was a scout ship that made an incursion, checked his bearings, and made another jump. This had been happening every fifteen minutes exactly for four weeks. Most likely recruits on training missions. Or some navigator royally pissed off an admiral, thought O'Shea.

When the next incursion happened at exactly thirteen minutes and eighteen seconds instead of fifteen minutes, O'Shea checked her chron again. Then she noticed a second incursion forming in the same general area. She reached to slap an alert button. By the time she did, five more incursions had appeared on her monitor. The alert sounded and brought the rest of the station to active alert. Her scope showed clearly that these ships coming through were *not* of human origin.

By the time the alert klaxon had sounded for the fifth time the scout ship had made its regular appearance. It observed what was happening and stayed only for the few seconds required to recharge the jump engines. By then, twenty-nine other incursions into normal space had occurred.

Chief O'Shea was explaining to her superior about the incursions when the number reached four hundred.

By the time her superior got over his shock and sounded the system wide alarm, the number was over one thousand and still growing. O'Shea was now engaged in prayer, attempting to "make peace with her maker." Something that people all over the system were doing as they observed the incoming war fleet.

In an odd manifestation, no two ships had ever met in null space. It had been hypothetically proven that no two ever could, even when leaving the same location at the same time and traveling to the same destination. But, ships could communicate amongst each other while in null space. They could not, however, communicate with anyone or anything in normal space.

The scout ship Farragut made the incursion back into null space for the two hundred eighty fourth time without any physical harm, but with her crew somewhat shaken this time around. They had just witnessed a horrifying sight. An enormous war fleet invading the capital system of the CHC.

The newly promoted second lieutenant in charge of both science and communications looked somewhat gray in pallor. Although stressed and scared to the point of nearly befouling his pants, he followed his orders to the letter.

"Confirm Binqk ships in those incursions," he spoke aloud to his commander.

"I confirm incursions with Binqk ships entering normal space 4725 Cancri system," the first officer responded. "Transmit to Fleet Commander. I repeat. Confirm incursions and incoming Binqk fleet. Transmit to Fleet Commander then wake the Captain and get her up here."

The Lieutenant pressed a stud on the communications console and transmitted a pre-recorded message coded for Admiral Brave Eagle.

Eight seconds passed before Admiral Brave Eagle responded to the message.

"Sir," the Lieutenant reported to the first officer. "I have an audio only link with Admiral Brave Eagle."

"Put him on," the first officer ordered. At a gesture from his communications officer he said, "Go ahead, Admiral."

"Report!" Admiral Brave Eagle ordered rather succinctly.

"Sir. Upon our last incursion into the 4725 Cancri system we observed immense quantities of incursions. We matched the ships coming through the incursions with the energy signatures and vessel profiles in our ship's database. They are definitely of Binqk origin."

"Thank you, Commander." Admiral Brave Eagle said as he closed the connection.

# CHAPTER 33

Aboard the Bismarck, Captain Alexi Andreiovich was hurrying to the bridge. The alert had come while he was off duty and in the shower. But he knew without a doubt exactly what the only thing that could cause the alert would be.

Captain Andreiovich flew through the hatchway and onto the bridge his hair still wet and with just a few soap bubbles clinging to it. "Report, Number One," he ordered as he maneuvered into his command couch with its wrap-around console.

"I have Admiral Brave Eagle on comm link for you, Captain." Commander Farmer responded crisply. "Transfer now."

A screen lit up in front of the captain. Admiral Jefferson Brave Eagle's face looked out of the screen. "Captain Andreiovich, it has begun. You are to take your battle group and the second and third carrier group and make the incursion into normal space. There you will engage the enemy. We will send a fleet of one battle group and two carrier groups every two minutes until this thing is over, one way or another. Good luck Alexi. We'll see you on the other side."

"Thank you Admiral. Good luck to you also, Sir. I look forward to you buying me a beer when this whole thing is over. Andreiovich out. Comm, patch me into our fleet," he ordered.

A light on the Captain's command console showed the communications channel as live. The Captain flipped a switch as he sat up straighter. "This is Captain Andreiovich to the First Fleet. Binqk attack is confirmed. Red alert status, prepare for incursion to normal space. All fighter pilots to virtual flight bays and stand ready to launch fighters immediately after the incursion. All capital ships show ready status to make incursion."

Toggling the switch again the Captain turned to his own crew and barked, "Warm up all weapons, all reactors to full power. Bring defensive grid online. Ready the jump engines to make the incursion. Let me know when the rest of the fleet is ready."

"Weapons hot and ready, Sir!"

"Reactors running at maximum output, Sir."

"Defensive grid coming online now. Full tactical display available."

"Jump engines ready."

"The fleet shows ready Captain."

Captain Andreiovich toggled the switch again. "All ships! Incursion into normal space in five seconds from my mark."

A computerized voice started a count, "Five, four, three, two, one, incursion now."

Billions of stars swirled around both inside and outside the ship. Captain Andreiovich found himself both everywhere and nowhere at the same time. He had the strange impression that he was inside out. He heard an odd popping noise accompanied by the sensation that his ears had popped, except that the sensation was throughout his entire body.

Then he was looking at a screen in front of him. Displayed on it was the incursion and through it a limited view of the system they were entering. There were far too many Binqk ships there for Alexi Andreiovich's liking.

Captain Andreiovich had fully expected to come through the incursion while Binqk gunners used his ships for target practice. Being totally ignored had never crossed his mind. In retrospect, he might have expected as much. When you have a fleet this large entering a system one hardly expects a much smaller enemy fleet to show up in the middle of your own incoming ships.

Captain Andreiovich, being a quick thinker, took immediate advantage of the situation.

"Helm take us directly between that carrier and that cruiser dead ahead. All weapons prepare for double broadside salvos. Main forward batteries and rail guns target that carrier just past them. Hold your fire if you please. I want all three targets hit at the same time. Steady gunners. Steady. And . . . Fire!"

All three Binqk ships were caught totally unprepared. The Bismarck port and starboard gunners had raked their two targets at pointblank range with particle beam cannons, x-ray laser cannons, mini-rail guns throwing one hundred kilos of high explosives, and six torpedoes per side. The two ships did not suffer long. Within a mere handful of seconds, they both exploded into little more than plasma and gas.

The third ship, another carrier, took a tremendous blow when a two—kiloton mass from the Bismarck's primary rail gun slammed into it. Her hull nearly split in two, her launch bay was destroyed along with her landing bays. The majority of her crew were dead from explosive decompression. One lone torpedo lanced out and pierced the dying carrier. Seconds later she exploded in a blinding flash as her fusion drive went supercritical.

There was no time for celebrating aboard the Bismarck. Captain Andreiovich was gathering his small fleet together and taking out as many Binqk as possible before they realized what was happening.

"The second wave of our ships is making the incursion Captain," Commander Farmer reported.

The Bismarck rocked as an enemy missile detonated against the armor plating of her hull. The hull groaned its protest.

There were explosions going on all over the general vicinity. Ships from both human and Binqk fleets constantly making the incursion. The combined DES/CHC fleet launched nearly three thousand cyberfighters. They were tearing into the Binqk ships almost at will, wreaking havoc and mayhem at such high speeds that even the anti-fighter batteries on the Binqk ships could not hit them. Confusion ran high throughout the Binqk fleet.

"Andreiovich to First Fleet. Binqk ships coming through an incursion are unaware of our presence. Attack the ships coming through incursions where possible. They do not have their defenses up yet."

# CHAPTER 34

Admiral Eenvupe knew something was drastically wrong at the other end of the communications link. The Emperor's communications officer looked fearful for its life. The Emperor was going to watch the battle via pickups on Eenvupe's ship, which was not too abnormal, but the Binqk Leader usually wanted more 'direct' information. The dangerously calm manner in which the Emperor had informed Eenvupe that it would watch, using Eenvupe's ship for a viewpoint, raised the minor appendages on Admiral Eenvupe's upper torso.

The Emperor was not known for being subtle or calm.

Whatever was wrong that put the Emperor in such a foul mood, Eenvupe knew it had better not allow anything here to add kindling to the fire of the Emperor's nasty temper. Its life would most likely be forfeit if it did.

"Progress report," snapped Eenvupe.

The science officer looked up and responded. "Fleet deployment progressing as expected. No engagements so far. There is a small fleet of around one hundred and fifty human fighter craft heading from three of the space based stations to intercept us. We anticipate fifty-seven minutes before they achieve weapons range. We are detecting more fighter craft being launched from various locations throughout the system. We have identified at least twelve and possibly as many as fourteen capital ships in this system—nothing this fleet cannot handle, Admiral."

"Do not permit yourself to get a superior attitude," Eenvupe warned. "Such things allow us to make poor choices now that will haunt us from now until the afterlife."

"I serve your orders Admiral," the science officer groveled.

Eenvupe raised its voice in anger, "You serve your Emperor! You merely follow Its orders through me."

"Forgive my error. It is my sole duty to serve my Emperor through your orders." The science officer was prepared to continue groveling after its faux pas with the admiral, when its station started beeping for attention.

"Admiral!" the science officer nearly shrieked, "I have detected explosions within the fleet."

"What?" demanded Admiral Eenvupe.

"Two, no three ships are exploding. More explosions! Eleven ships are now nothing but plasma. Sixteen more have taken heavy damage from weapons fire. Admiral, there is a small fleet of human ships making incursions within close proximity and attacking our fleet! And it looks like more human ships coming through incursions in amongst our fleet! The ships they already sent have also managed to launch approximately one thousand fighter craft!

"Your orders Admiral?" its first officer whined.

Admiral Eenvupe felt like whining too. This was not how the battle was supposed to go. Being the one responsible for both the outcome of the battle and any explanations for it, good or bad, Eenvupe was all too aware that no Binqk, especially not the Emperor, would understand the human phrase, "Don't kill the messenger."

Katy O'Shea had finished up her prayers as quickly as possible. Her duties now required her complete attention. She had already acknowledged that she was going to die this day, as were all the people she had ever known on the planet she was sworn to protect. And now doing her duty was going to help make those responsible pay as dear a price as possible for that carnage.

The quantity of these alien ships was astounding, over four thousand and still coming. She was just about to report the newest count to the station's commodore when something on the scope caught her eye.

"Commodore! I am picking up multiple explosions inside the enemy fleet!"

"Confirm! Multiple explosions inside enemy fleet?" the Commodore ordered.

"Confirmed!" came the response from three stations at once.

"What is causing them? Our ships are nowhere near firing range yet."

"I read forty ships out there that appear to be human built," Chief O'Shea said.

"Appear to be?" The commodore responded. "Are they or are they not human ships, Chief?"

"Sir this cannot be right. My scope must be malfunctioning."

"Explain! But be damn quick about it," snapped the Commodore."

"Commodore these ships look similar in design to both our ships and to ships of the DES but they appear to be neither. Yet they fly the colors of both. And I have a transponder signal from one of them declaring it as the CHC Fredericksburg. Sir, the Fredericksburg was destroyed over a month ago. I should remember. My mother was her third officer."

"Commodore!" another ensign called for attention. "I have identified eight transponder signals for CHC ships that have been reported as destroyed, three more for ships belonging to the DES that have also been reported as destroyed."

"What the hell's going on here?" the Commodore said half to himself.

"Sir!" another ensign called. "I show forty more of the same type of ships starting an attack run on the aliens and launching an impossible number of cyberfighters. Sir, their cyberfighters are tearing the enemy fleet to shreds. But where could they get all those cyber pilots?"

"How many cyberfighters do you count?" asked the Commodore.

"Somewhere in the neighborhood of two thousand."

"What!" demanded the Commodore. "I doubt there are that many cyber pilots in both the CHC and DES combined."

"Yes Sir," the ensign said noncommittally, "but nevertheless Sir, there they are."

"Commodore, I show another forty of those ships now in the system. They are launching even more cyberfighters and starting an attack run," O'Shea informed him.

"Who the hell are they?" the Commodore asked no one in particular.

"A hoax of some kind," O'Shea muttered.

"Ensign?" the Commodore inquired.

"A hoax," she said louder. "We have been the victims of a hoax. It is the only explanation."

"Explain!" the Commodore ordered.

"Praise be to Allah!" she exclaimed as full realization dawned. "Sir! It is the only thing that makes sense! Somehow the big brass got wind of this alien invasion. They cooked up a war between us and the DES as an excuse to build more ships. Then they would 'lose' a ship or two in a battle and the ship would go somewhere to get refurbished and is now part of that fleet out there."

"Chief," the Commodore said seriously, "that is probably the craziest and most asinine thing I have ever heard. Which is all the more reason that I believe it likely to be true." Smiling he added, "A very nice bit of reasoning Katy. Warn all of our ships and stations not to fire on those vessels unless fired upon first."

"Sir, Commodore!" another ensign called excitedly.

"Yes," the Commodore responded calmly.

"Six alien capital ships have left their fleet and are headed for the planet."

"Launch all our remaining cyberfighters and our manned fighters as well. And somebody get me a tube of coffee. It looks like this might be a long day unless it ends very abruptly. Either way I could use the caffeine. Let's go people!"

Captain Alexi Andreiovich was pressed painfully into the restraints on his command couch as two more missiles slammed into the Bismarck.

"Damage report!" he demanded.

"Number four shield gone. Minor damage to armor on deck seven. We have also lost the armor protecting decks eight and nine, sections D through F," responded the lieutenant at the engineering console.

"Captain," first officer David Farmer said, "I have detected a group of vessels breaking away from the enemy fleet and heading for either the planet or the Lagrange space stations."

"How many Number One?" asked the Captain.

"Six of their cruisers and four of their battleships, Sir."

"Send two cyber squadrons to keep them busy for now. Then contact the Herbert Hoover, the George Bush, and the George Custer. We will rendezvous en route. The four of us are going to tackle those ships before they can hit the planet or the station."

"Aye Sir," Farmer responded.

Touching the stud on his command console for a pre-set comm link, Captain Andreiovich leaned back and stretched. A screen on his console came alive with the features of Admiral Brave Eagle.

"Yes Captain?" asked the face on the screen as it shook from a hit by the aliens.

"Admiral, we have detected a group of six Binqk cruisers and two battleships headed for the planet. I intend to take the Hoover, the Bush, and the Custer to intercept. My carriers might need a little extra cover fire without us if the Binqk detect it as a weak spot."

"Very good Alexi. I'll do everything in my power to keep them safe. You just do the same for that planet," Admiral Brave Eagle said seriously, "and I think it would be prudent to send a carrier with you." The Admiral grinned at some private joke and continued, "I think I have just the one for you," he added merrily. Then he made several hand gestures to someone off screen. "She just came through and has not launched any of her fighters. I am sending her your transponder codes and orders now. Brave Eagle out."

Alexi was in no mood to argue about having the extra firepower of a carrier and her two hundred cyberfighters going along to help protect the planet and space stations. He wondered about the Admiral's private joke though. Brave Eagle was not known for having a sense of humor.

One hour and twelve minutes later, the last of the tiny fleet of five ships, the only carrier in the small fleet, caught up and came into formation en route to protect the planet and the Lagrange point space stations. There were thirty-two minutes left before interception of the Binqk ships headed to the planet unless the fighters managed to stop the eight enemy craft.

The allied carrier's hull was flying the flags of both the CHC and DES, the same as the rest of the new fleet, but she also had a third flag, it sported a large circular hoop made of one branch complete with leaves and in the hoop were a longbow with an arrow bearing a stone tip in the middle. The ship's name was Sitting Bull.

Captain Alexi Andreiovich laughed out loud. Being a student of history, he understood Admiral Brave Eagle's private joke. He vowed when this was over, and the admiral and he could get together, he would buy Brave Eagle a drink, be it the best Denebian brandy or a simple root beer float. Alexi had not the slightest idea what the admiral preferred, but he knew one thing without a doubt. This time he owed the admiral a drink.

Now that their small fleet was together they could all make a full three-gravity acceleration. The ships could handle more, even the crew could handle more for short periods. However, even battle hardened and space experienced troops could only handle three gravities and still be able to fight at the end of the trip. The greater the acceleration, the less time and functionality the troops would have at the end of traverse. After that, there developed a tremendous diminishing return curve. The five human ships continued accelerating in system at three gravities to intercept the eight Binqk vessels.

Cyber squadrons based in the system had hit the Binqk ships hard and were heading back to refuel. However, they had done their job exceedingly well before they left. They forced the Binqk attack fleet to turn and face the human fleet rather than damaging Memory Beta or her satellites. They also cost the aliens one for certain and possibly two, capital ships.

The second damaged alien ship was still accelerating toward the planet. She displayed no other signs of power output other than her stellar drive. Not one single light burned anywhere visible. She showed no signs of life. The remaining four alien ships were facing the "V" shaped menace that was the incoming human fleet.

Leading the small human fleet was the Bismarck. Captain Alexi Andreiovich barked out orders. "We will be in weapons range of the Binqk ships in eighteen seconds. Once we are within range all weapons fire two rounds on that lead ship, then fire at will."

"Captain!" the first officer called. "More Binqk ships have broken away from the main fleet and are headed towards the planet!"

"How many this time, Number One?" Andreiovich asked.

There was a slight catch in his voice as Commander Farmer responded, "Three hundred, Sir."

"Understood," the Captain growled. Then he re-opened the communications link with Admiral Brave Eagle.

"Yes Alexi," came the slightly distracted response.

"Admiral, I have detected a large group of ships breaking away from the main fleet and headed this way."

"Yes, we detected them too. The next two fleets to make the incursion will head your way. In the meantime I am sending another fifty ships to you. You are to take command of that fleet and defend Memory Beta at all costs. For now though you will just have to hold out by yourselves." The Admiral's ship rocked under a tremendous impact.

"Understood Admiral, Andreiovich out."

"All gunners fire at will," commanded the first officer. The Captain looked up at the main screen just in time to see the Binqk ships open fire.

This time they used a new tactic. All four remaining ships concentrated their fire on the Bismarck.

The great battleship rocked and pitched under the combined firepower of the four Binqk ships. Her electronic shielding overheated and began to give out. Her ablative armor was all but burned away. The immense hull cried out in protest against the explosive forces it was required to endure.

Yet the Binqk ships continued to fire until forced to re-target the other human ships or be destroyed.

An acrid stench and smoke filled the bridge. That and the sickly sweet odor of singed flesh. People were crying out in pain. The only light was from three consoles, one that seemed fine, and two that flickered off and on and occasionally spit sparks.

"Report!" Captain Andreiovich yelled into the dark.

"Decks eight and nine sections A and B are gone, sections C through G are exposed to vacuum. Defensive grid, offline. Weapons systems, offline. Navigation systems, offline. Sensors, limited passive systems only. Life support systems, offline. Communications . . . Dear God!" the first officer exclaimed.

"What is it, Dave?" the Captain inquired politely.

"The entire communications panel exploded. I saw no one in the seat so I sat down to check out the panel. I sat down on the lower half of Ensign Walker. The upper half was removed when the panel exploded."

Captain Alexi Andreiovich could think of nothing to reply to that so he simply said, "Please continue with the damage report, Number One."

"Aye Captain," Commander Farmer answered uncertainly. But he continued, "Uhm, communications are totally out. Stellar drive functioning at one hundred percent."

In response to the report the captain touched a stud on his command console. "Captain to Environmental Engineering."

"Meier here, Captain."

"How long until life support can be restored Mr. Meier?"

"Captain, I am not sure it can be restored. May I have five minutes for damage inspection, Sir?"

"You have two minutes mister! Captain out."

"Dave see if you can get navigation back online. I will try getting the sensors working."

Two minutes later a chime sounded on the captain's command console. Andreiovich moved to the console and touched a stud. "Yes?" he said simply.

"Captain this is Meier in Environmental Engineering" a voice said. "I have that report you wanted."

"Go ahead."

"Sir, I can probably get the life support working again. I estimate thirty minutes or never. However, I cannot guarantee more than fifty percent capabilities. We have quite a bit of damage down here."

"Understood, thank you Lieutenant" the Captain said.

"Uh, that's Ensign Meier Sir." the voice responded.

"Very well Ensign. Would you mind explaining why your lieutenant did not respond to my call?"

"Because she is dead Sir," came the response.

"I see. Very well Lieutenant. Carry on," the Captain acknowledged.

"Sir? It's Ensign Meier."

"Lieutenant Meier. I expect you to fulfill the duties of your new rank. Get your people working down there and get that life support system up and running as soon as possible or sooner!"

"Aye Sir, but there is one more thing."

"Yes Lieutenant, what is it?" the Captain inquired impatiently.

"Sir, even with only half the crew still alive, given the airtight space left on this ship, we are all going to run out of air in about twenty minutes."

"Yes, I had thought about that also. Keep doing what you can to get the life support repaired. I have a plan. Captain out."

Captain Alexi Andreiovich touched another stud on his command console. This one gave him ship wide announcement ability.

"Attention all hands. This is the captain. Shortly this ship will run out of breathable air. We will not be able to reestablish life support prior to that time. It is my plan to have this ship fighting again. To do that, I need to have life support. My immediate strategy is to have the majority of the crew abandon ship. If we cut down to minimal crew we will have enough air to repair life support. This means I am going to order all of you other than command crew and environmental engineering not to abandon ship, but to leave and take up the fight elsewhere. You will be leaving by shuttle and escape pod. First, I would like to explain something. The rest of our tiny fleet will be able to easily pick everyone up. Any ship in this fleet that picks you up is bound to have taken, or will take in the near future, casualties. Therefore, you will still get the chance to fight just from another ship. And by leaving the Bismarck you give her the best chance to live and fight again. I will ask for volunteers to stay on this ship to fight and make repairs. The rest will leave immediately. I repeat, the rest will leave the ship immediately. To those of you who stay, Commander Farmer will be taking command of the Bismarck. Thank you." the Captain finished.

"Captain?" asked Commander Farmer.

"Dave, I have command responsibilities to this fleet that supersede the command of this ship. I will transfer my flag to the Sitting Bull, and take command of the fleet. You will stay, take command of the Bismarck, and get her ready to fight again."

"Understood Captain," Farmer responded.

"Dave, seriously. This is my ship. We have been through a lot together. Now, I am entrusting *you* to take command and bring her home at the end of the day."

"Sir!" Farmer saluted smartly even if he sounded choked up. "I promise I'll bring her home or die trying, Sir."

# CHAPTER 35

Admiral Eenvupe of the Binqk Empire was trying to explain to its emperor how they could be losing a battle where they had the enemy ships outnumbered nearly five to one.

"We cannot compete with their fighter craft, my Liege. They seem to ignore the laws of physics! These craft accelerate at up to one hundred fifty gravities. They perform turns and maneuvers that would be certain death to our pilots. We do not understand how their pilots live through this but most of the craft seem too small to have a pilot on board anyway. Yet, there must be because they are definitely under a pilot's control.

"They dodge our fighters with ease. They attack our capital ships unmolested. Our gunners can target them but cannot get a hit, and even our computers are unable to track them, they are so swift. My Liege, we must withdraw our forces. We have already lost nearly two thousand capital ships and their crews. Another one thousand ships are heavily damaged. Most of our fighter craft are destroyed."

"Arrrr!" the Emperor roared its anger.

Eenvupe watched on the screen as the Emperor lifted a hand filled with something the Admiral could not see.

There was the sound of a high-energy discharge from a hand weapon, immediately followed by the "krump" noise of a body hitting the floor. Eenvupe had no doubts it had just witnessed the fate awaiting it, if it lived to report in person to the emperor. Even so Eenvupe pressed on, "My Liege, we must withdraw. Our current predictions based on the battle so far show us winning but with less than three hundred surviving ships."

"No!" screamed the Emperor. "Admiral you were given all of the equipment and knowledge to wipe out that system and that is exactly what you are going to do. If you die doing so, it will be a much quicker and simpler death than if you or your crews run from this battle."

"*I understand*, my Liege. Then I must return my attention to the battle. Eenvupe out."

Eenvupe believed what the emperor had said about the fate awaiting admirals or crewmen that left this battle.

Calling from its ready room to the bridge, Eenvupe ordered the captain of the ship to join it in the ready room. "Hutspa," the Admiral began, "our estimates of the battle show us winning but with less than three hundred ships left. What is your recommendation?"

"Admiral, I am not in command of this mission," Hutspa seemed confused. "Why would you need my opinion?"

"I am quite aware of who is in command. Just answer the question."

"Admiral, I would then recommend an immediate withdrawal."

"Excellent Hutspa. The Emperor has promised that any of us who run from this battle will be put to a slow death. Yet if we fight, we can only win at the cost of five thousand more ships and their crews. Even then we cannot hope to achieve the goals of this assault on the humans. I need to know if you will work with me Hutspa, I need to know if you will help me save Binqk lives and our remaining ships. Can I count on you?"

"Admiral I am no coward. But avoiding the useless waste of lives and material is not cowardice. What do you need me to do?"

"First, the emperor is watching the battle through our sensors. We need to shut down its communications link. Make that look like an accident, or battle damage. Once this is accomplished, we can go anywhere without the emperor knowing."

"How soon do you want me to shut off the link Admiral?" asked Hutspa.

Take what time you need to make it sufficiently convincing. But remember, the longer it takes the more Binqk lives will be lost in this useless confrontation."

"Understood Admiral."

From the vantage point of Lagrange Station Number Five, it was an incredible battle to watch. Chief O'Shea was grateful however, that she had not had an opportunity to participate in it.

She watched as a human fleet of approximately three thousand capital ships from the combined DES/CHC forces battled a fleet of over eight thousand alien capital ships.

The humans were prevailing only due to the effectiveness of the cyberfighters.

A smaller alien fleet of three hundred ships had broken off the main conflict and headed for the planet.

They were being intercepted by a fleet of one hundred thirty human ships. The human ships were mostly carriers. Formidable on their own, they each carried two hundred cyberfighters which tipped the scale a bit in the humans' favor.

Ships were exploding in violent flashes nearly everywhere O'Shea looked. Then she noticed an alien ship make a course correction that was taking it straight towards the station.

Two cyberfighters were all over the Binqk vessel trying to force her to make a course change. They pounded the alien ship again and again.

Suddenly O'Shea realized the collision alarm was screaming for attention. Without thinking, and by shear repetition of training, she leapt from her post and headed towards the nearest life pod. She was looking for anyone following her, when she heard a tremendous tearing and screeching noise as tortured metal flew apart.

O'Shea's entire world started shaking dramatically. Just as she entered the pod, her ears popped and the hatch automatically slammed shut and locked. Inside she was brutally tossed about.

Then everything went still. She heard a pounding on the hatch and looked up. There was the commodore. His eyes were bulging; his nose, mouth, and ears bleeding. He gave one last weak knock on the pod's hatch then stopped moving and slowly drifted away. Katy O'Shea fastened the safety straps on her seat and launched the life pod into space.

Aboard the carrier Sitting Bull, Captain Black Elk called to Captain Andreiovich. "Captain Andreiovich, I think you had better have a look at this."

Captain Alexi Andreiovich came to see what Captain Black Elk was referring to. Andreiovich looked into the monitor to see the Bismarck on a course projected to ram the Binqk ship that was flying with a dead stick. "What in the hell . . . ?" Alexi exclaimed.

"Captains!" The young woman at science announced. "According to the computer estimate of its present course, the Binqk ship with the dead stick will burrow straight into the planet in the middle of the heaviest population centers of the Northern continent, at a relative velocity of point three C."

"At that velocity it would be like someone dropped a thousand fusion bombs on the planet," Black Elk commented, the horror clear in his voice.

"Communications, can you raise the Bismarck?" Andreiovich requested.

"Negative Sir. No response," came the reply.

"Damn!" Andreiovich swore. "Can we get enough cyberfighters there in time to blast that Binqk ship to hell?"

"Negative Captain," Black Elk answered. "They don't have the firepower to blow it into small enough pieces to do any good. Only if they accidentally hit a fusion reactor causing just the right damage to result in it going supercritical."

"There has to be another way to stop that ship," Alexi mumbled.

Captain Robert Black Elk placed his hand gently on the shoulder of Captain Andreiovich and said softly, "Alexi, there is no other way to save the planet in time. The Bismarck may just have to be another casualty of this battle. At least she is dying for a good cause."

"Captains!" came the young ensign sitting at the communications board. "I have Admiral Brave Eagle requesting to speak to Captain Andreiovich."

"On my monitor if you please, Ms. Charger," Captain Black Elk ordered.

"Captain Andreiovich!" Admiral Brave Eagle sounded elated. "The Binqk fleet is retreating. They are making incursions as fast as they can get safe from immediate fire."

Captain Black Elk looked to science station one where an ensign caught the unspoken order and checked the validity of this claim.

The Admiral continued, "We are letting them retreat from our capital ships but are pressing them as hard as we can with the cyberfighters."

The ensign at science station one looked back at his captain and nodded confirmation of the statement.

"That is good news Sir," Captain Andreiovich answered. "But I have an immediate situation here I need to deal with. Is there anything else, Sir?"

"Yes," Brave Eagle said slowly. "I have received data on what the Bismarck is doing. Would your 'situation' have something to do with stopping her?"

"Admiral, I . . . Sir! The Bismarck is my ship, Sir."

"Captain Andreiovich. The Bismarck is not your ship, Sir! You relinquished your command of her to Commander Farmer." Then changing tack, "Alexi, I know how hard it is to lose a ship. I have had one shot right out from under me and had another's fusion reactor go supercritical because of battle damage. "We had to abandon her and watch helplessly as she blew up. Now, if the Bismarck survives this you can have her back. For now though, your responsibilities are still with your fleet. The Bismarck may be part of that fleet but she is still Commander Farmer's ship for now."

"Yes Admiral," Alexi said with a lump in his throat. "Will that be all for now, Sir?" he asked.

"No, one more thing. I want you to fall back with your capital ships and press the Binqk as hard as you can."

"Aye, aye, Sir. You can count on me, Admiral. Andreiovich out."

Turning from the monitor, Captain Andreiovich said, "Captain Black Elk, I already sit in your command couch to run the fleet. I could use one spare ensign from a science station and enough of the communications officer's time as available, if you would be so kind as to see about talking a maniac out of destroying my ship."

"Captain Andreiovich, it would be my pleasure to do anything I can to help save your ship, Sir." Black Elk said earnestly. "Though I believe your Commander Farmer is doing the correct thing."

"Captain Andreiovich," barked the ensign at science station three. "The Binqk ships are retreating. Orders, Sir?"

"All ships follow but stay out of weapons range. Allow the Binqk ships to withdraw from our capital ships. Our fighters are to press them hard. Make them pay for every single one of their ships that gets away. Make them pay for every single human who died here today."

# CHAPTER 36

Admiral Eenvupe had taken the step. The step from which it knew there was no return. The emperor had been insane with rage. Permission was refused. And Eenvupe had made the most difficult decision of its entire career. In order to save Binqk lives Eenvupe had ordered the fleet to withdraw, make an incursion as soon as it was safe, and rendezvous at a star on the edge of Binqk space.

After the first three thousand Binqk ships made the incursion to null space, Eenvupe left the 4725 Cancri system. They passed safely into the incursion. Then Admiral Eenvupe left the bridge for its office. There was a speech to write. The fleet had to know of their new status, but not until they were all safe. It had a few hours yet.

Chief Katy O'Shea sat in the life pod transfixed with the scene unfolding outside. One of the alien ships was headed on a course that looked like it might go straight into the planet below.

Coming in from an angle, but so close she felt sure it was going to ram her life pod, was one of those strange human ships with the markings of both the CHC and the DES. It appeared to be headed straight for the alien.

Both ships were obviously heavily damaged. Neither showed any sign of life or control.

Katy's life pod had somehow been damaged during her launch and the following explosion. There was no operational radio or transponder. She had maneuvering thrusters but no drive.

The planet that seemed so close she could reach out and touch was nearly two days away. And even then, she could not land. Right now though, her attention was rooted on the battleship passing so close to her life pod. She saw the many protrusions of the ship coming at her. Each time a new projection passed, it looked like it was the one that would reach out and crush her tiny pod. When the largest protrusion passed she let out the breath she did not realize she had been holding.

That is when the universe around her jumped violently and she was pressed painfully into her safety harness. At the same time, there was a terribly loud gong noise accompanied by another sound similar to a ground vehicle crash but without the breaking glass.

Katy found she could not breathe. She was certain the hull had been breached by part of the battleship. But, as the effects of the impact and subsequent rapid acceleration desisted, she found that there was indeed air to breathe. There was now a huge dent on the top of the life pod.

She looked out the view port to see another life pod tumbling away, its drive a crushed useless mess. Quickly she used her thrusters to chase after the damaged pod.

All of a sudden a brilliant light lit up the sky as the two capital ships, one alien and one human, collided with a tremendous explosion.

The human vessel hit the alien amidships and nearly cut her in half; the remaining parts of the alien's fore and aft sections wrapping around her aggressor.

But it was at the cost of the forward two-thirds of the human ship's mass. Most of the remaining portion was mixed into the tangled mess of the alien ship. That was when the fusion reactors on both craft went supercritical.

The life pod's view port automatically darkened in microseconds to protect the occupants' eyes. But it also stayed dark and left the pilot without an external view for nearly three seconds.

When she could finally see, Katy found herself right on top of the other life pod. It had nearly stopped tumbling so someone was alive and at the controls.

She matched course and speed while the pilot of the other life pod stopped the tumbling. As soon as the tumbling stopped, she docked with the other pod.

After opening her hatch she found the other pod's portal still secured. They had to have felt the bump as she docked. Deciding the person or persons inside might have been hurt when the two life pods collided, she went ahead and unlatched the other hatch.

Floating into the other life pod, she discovered one occupant, male, with commanders' pips on a uniform that had markings of both the CHC and DES. And it was quite obvious he was injured.

Half dried blood was smeared across his face and scalp. He was dirty and covered with soot and ash. His left arm had a bandage that was soaked with blood. The right arm was obviously broken. There was a large burn on the right side of his lower ribs and a gash on his forehead. He had a large bump on the back of his head that appeared to be from the couch he was improperly strapped into. He was unconscious.

Immediately, she retrieved the med kit and proceeded to tend his wounds.

Captain Alexi Andreiovich watched the last surviving Binqk ship enter an incursion and get away.

Then he flipped his monitor to another channel and watched as the Bismarck rammed the Binqk ship headed for Memory Beta.

Captain Black Elk had attempted to contact the Bismarck a dozen or more times. He tried standard subspace frequencies, emergency frequencies, and communications lasers on a tight beam. Even radio signals failed.

As Black Elk told Captain Andreiovich, "I tried everything but smoke signals. No response."

"No smoke signals?" Andreiovich said halfheartedly.

"I haven't yet managed to get a fire to burn in space," Black Elk said with mock seriousness.

"Well you have my profound thanks anyway Captain." Andreiovich informed him.

"And you have my profound sympathies for the loss of your ship, Captain," Black Elk returned sincerely. Andreiovich nodded a thanks and turned his attention back to his duty.

"Communications get me Memory Beta approach control. I am sure they have a lot of questions for us."

Aboard its flagship, Admiral Eenvupe, formerly of the Binqk Empire, addressed the remains of its fleet, somewhere around four thousand five hundred ships.

"Binqk of the Imperial First Fleet," Eenvupe began.

"All of our best predictions showed that less than three hundred ships would survive the battle had we continued. When it was over, we would not have been able to achieve our objectives; we would have merely thrown away your lives.

"It is my unpleasant duty to inform you that I disobeyed direct orders from the emperor when we retreated from the humans. I chose not to throw away your lives to save the emperor's face and ego.

"Consequently, we are all under sentence of death from the emperor for leaving the battle.

"Therefore, it is my duty to make sure you understand the nature of what we have become. We cannot go back to the empire. We are outlaws. But since we are outlaws I suggest we do what outlaws do to survive.

"Of course, by our strict military tradition, you need to take a captain's vote as to whether I am fit to command this fleet. If the fleet captains would care to make their vote, I will await your decision. Admiral Eenvupe out."

# CHAPTER 37

Seven days after the battle at 4725 Cancri:

DES Starship 1 hung close by the Presidential carrier CHC Alabama.

Aboard the Alabama a small informal gathering was taking place.

"Ally, you look ravishing," President Lao Chin was saying to President Allison McCallister.

"Lao, I will bet ten credits you say that to all the girls," McCallister responded.

"You're on! Tserofed! Come here for a moment will you?"

"Oh now that is cheating," McCallister said.

"Are you saying that she is not a girl? Why, from what I have learned about Fombe customs, she would be happy to show you and prove you wrong right here and now."

"I have read the same reports. I know she would do exactly that. Fombe have no 'hang ups' about their bodies. And that was not what I meant and you damn well know it," McCallister retorted.

Across the room, Admiral Christopher Price came up behind both Hotchkins and Anuk as they stood facing Captain Andreiovich. Clearing his throat loudly he said, "Mr. Ambassadors if I may have a word?" Both men gave a start before turning around.

"Admiral Price!" they said in unison complete with silly grins on their faces.

"In here Chris will do," he said softly. "Well both of you two have done quite well for yourselves. Have you made any plans?"

Hotchkins looked at Anuk and answered first, "I am bound for the Fombe home world in three days. It seems we have a great deal of trade negotiations to work out."

"And I," said Anuk, "ship out tomorrow morning for the Pilok home world."

"In that case, gentlemen," Chris said, "we had better do our celebrating tonight."

President McCallister was casually scratching Bakstrah between his eyestalks while Bakstrah carried on a conversation with Captain Andreiovich.

"So your Commander Farmer saved millions of lives at the cost of his own?" Bakstrah was asking.

"Yes, he was quite a man. He endured five gravities of acceleration for six hours in order to get the angle and speed required to destroy that ship before it could do any damage to the planet. Apparently though, after that heavy acceleration for so long, he could not make it to the life pod. At least there was no transponder signal from one and they could not physically locate a pod."

"Quite a hero indeed," Bakstrah responded, "he should be well honored."

"And do not fret Captain," McCallister said with a wink. "I am sure that eventually you might be trusted with another ship."

"Ally," Lao Chin was saying, "I cannot believe we pulled it off."

"Neither can I. But we both know that we just plain got lucky," President McCallister reminded him.

"Oh yes," Lao replied, "don't I know it. But for now at least we don't have to worry about the Binqk."

Bakstrah overheard that comment and sauntered over to the conversation.

"Excuse me I could not help but overhear your comment about the Binqk, Lao."

"You think they will attack again after the way we trashed them last week?" Lao Chin asked.

"You can count on it Sir," Bakstrah informed them. "As you know, the Binqk Emperor Pishmah Umselat Bourbaitoo III was deposed and killed within fifteen of your hours after its fleets were defeated and fled. This does not disqualify the Binqk from attempting to pursue this war. It is extremely popular with Binqk citizens, in spite of the tremendous losses they have suffered so far.

"All that aside, you have only met a fraction of their available military force, perhaps as little as twenty-five percent. They will continue to try, have no doubt about it.

"And you must be aware that sooner or later they are bound to discover your cyber technology. The Binqk may not be any good at developing or inventing technology, but they can copy and adapt it to their own needs quite well."

Things were winding down in the small group. It had been an extremely hectic year for them all right up until today. As they de-stressed, relaxed, and "let their hair down" they grew quieter and found themselves sinking deeper into the luxurious couches than usual.

A peaceful but insistent chime started sounding on the small modest desk in the corner.

President Allison McCallister said a word generally reserved for use by sailors and those who drove cross-country haulers, as she got up and went to respond.

Touching a stud on the desk she managed to politely ask, "Yes?"

"Madam President, I have an important comm link for Captain Alexi Andreiovich from the Fredericksburg. Is he still there?" asked the communications officer.

"Yes he is here. Transfer the link to this terminal." Turning she hollered, "Alexi! Captain Andreiovich? You have an important call coming in."

Alexi wasted no time. "Thank you, Madam President," he said before turning to the monitor.

"Good day. Captain Andreiovich I presume?" said the barely familiar face on the screen.

"Good day Sir. I am Captain Andreiovich. And who might you be?"

"Captain Williams of the Fredericksburg. I was in your assault wing at the battle of 4725 Cancri, Sir."

"Of course, forgive me please," said Alexi hoping to himself that Captain Williams would get on with whatever this was about.

"No need for apologies Sir. Now, as to the reason I have called. I have some news that should be of the utmost interest to you."

"Please continue Captain," Alexi said politely before gritting his teeth.

"Well, Sir, we located two life pods today. They were docked with each other and had hidden from the sun to conserve energy by snuggling up to a large chunk of debris that used to be part of the Lagrange Point Five station. Inside were a Chief O'Shea and a Commander Farmer. Your Commander Farmer is down in our sick bay right now. But I felt you should be informed as soon as possible."

"Oh, yes of course! Thank you, Captain Williams!" Alexi said in all seriousness. "But I must ask why is he in your sick bay? Is it serious?"

Captain Williams laughed before responding. "We know he has a broken arm, a couple of deep cuts, and one serious burn. But I do not believe it will prove to be fatal," Williams chuckled that last part out.

Alexi wondered at the joke but could not help but follow through as the joker wanted.

"You seem quite sure of your diagnosis Captain. May I ask why?"

Captain Williams was obviously fighting to keep the grin off of his face as he said, "Captain, do you remember I said there were two life pods and two survivors? One survivor was your Commander Farmer. The other was Chief Katy O'Shea from the Lagrange station. When the rescue team from my ship arrived, the two life pods were not the only things *docked*."

The next morning Hotchkins went to see Anuk off to the Pilok home world.

"Well Anuk, old friend. I guess this is it. It will probably be years before we see each other again, if ever," Hotchkins said.

"No, I do not think so," Anuk replied. "A spirit came to me in a dream last night. He spoke of a triple threat. He told me we would be working closely together in the near future. I will say goodbye to you my friend. But we will meet again soon."

"Oh crap, Anuk. I thought you were over that mumbo jumbo stuff."

"Maybe I am and maybe I am not," Anuk said with a smile. "Goodbye Hotch."

"One more thing Anuk. What the hell is your first name? Almost twenty—seven years we've known each other and I still don't know your first name."

"Ask the spirits, my friend. Ask the spirits." With that, Anuk turned and boarded his shuttle to orbit and the ship waiting to take him to the Pilok home world.